BERNARD SHAW:
SEVEN ONE-ACT PLAYS

Also edited by Jeffery Tillett
SHAKESPEARE, SHERIDAN AND SHAW

EDITED BY JEFFERY TILLETT

Bernard Shaw: Seven One-Act Plays

HOW HE LIED TO HER HUSBAND
PASSION, POISON AND PETRIFACTION
THE SHEWING-UP OF BLANCO POSNET
THE GLIMPSE OF REALITY
THE DARK LADY OF THE SONNETS
AUGUSTUS DOES HIS BIT
ANNAJANSKA, THE BOLSHEVIK EMPRESS

HEINEMANN EDUCATIONAL
BOOKS LTD · LONDON

LONDON MELBOURNE TORONTO
SINGAPORE JOHANNESBURG
AUCKLAND IBADAN
HONG KONG NAIROBI

Published by
Heinemann Educational Books Ltd
48 Charles Street, Mayfair, London W.1
Printed in Great Britain by
Cox & Wyman Ltd, London, Fakenham and Reading

CONTENTS

I am by profession a playwright. I have been in practice since 1892. I am not an ordinary playwright in general practice. I am a specialist in immoral and heretical plays. My reputation has been gained by my persistent struggle to force the public to reconsider its morals. I write plays with the deliberate object of converting the nation to my opinion in these matters. I have no other effectual incentive to write plays, as I am not dependent on the theatre for my livelihood. If I were prevented from producing immoral and heretical plays, I should cease to write for the theatre, and propagate my views from the platform and through books.

G.B.S.

INTRODUCTION

George Bernard Shaw was born in Dublin on 26 July 1856, the son of an unsuccessful and irresponsible corn merchant, whose wife left him to earn her living as a teacher of singing in London, taking their two daughters with her. The young Shaw stayed with his father in lodgings – they had had to sell their house – and after leaving school at fifteen worked for a time with success in a land agent's office. But in 1876, at the age of twenty, he followed his mother to London determined to earn his living by his pen.

It was nearly ten years before he was earning anything worth-while from writing and he was supported during that period mainly by his mother. Of course, that was the great age of the English novel, and it was only natural that Shaw should first try his hand in that direction; but all five novels he wrote failed to find a publisher. In fact, it was not until he had made his name as a playwright that they were published at all; by then publishers were only too willing to accept *anything* he had written.

But Shaw did not spend all his time on writing. He was interested in social problems and started to take an active part in politics, addressing meetings, and joining the newly-formed Fabian Society which aimed at a gradual and non-violent change in Britain from capitalism to socialism. Social problems were later to figure prominently as themes of Shaw's plays; and he was never happier than when the centre of controversy, often being deliberately provocative.

Then quite suddenly success came his way. He was given a book to review by William Archer, himself a well-known reviewer, who was overworked at the time. This review led to further work for Shaw, and soon he was busy. He had found his *métier* – as a critic. In a short time he was art critic to one paper and – very successfully – music critic to another. The love of painting and music which he had learnt from his mother from an early age and his own critical judgement he was now putting to good use. His reputation grew rapidly, and in artistic and cultural circles his name was on everybody's lips; equally important, his financial troubles were now at an end.

In the early 1890s Shaw became drama critic to *The Saturday Review*. He had himself written a play in 1885 but it was not performed until 1892, and even then was not a commercial success. Entitled *Widowers' Houses*, it dealt with the slum problem in cities. He continued to write plays but at first they were published and *read* rather than performed, and they were read as much for their provocative Prefaces, stimulating discussions on the problems posed by the plays, as for their dramatic and witty content. The fact that they were intended to be read also explains Shaw's very detailed descriptions of his sets, and the comments which he made on his characters, not only on their appearance but on their personality too. In the plays that followed *Widowers' Houses* he attacked the 'romance' of war (in *Arms and the Man*), religious intolerance (in *The Devil's Disciple*), the medical profession (in *The Doctor's Dilemma*), modern Christianity (in *Androcles and the Lion*), bigotry (in his greatest play, *Saint Joan*) and 'accent' and class distinctions (in *Pygmalion*). In all Shaw wrote some fifty plays, each one tilting at some social wrong or slyly parading Shaw's views on this and that through the words and actions of the people on the stage. His plays were, in fact, propaganda. Perhaps that is why they were not successful at first; not until an audience was found that wanted intellectual drama – something that provoked them, made them think and argue, or touched their consciences. Actually he was not doing anything new; the novelists, particularly Charles Dickens, had been doing this sort of thing for years, and the Norwegian dramatist Ibsen had also used the stage to ventilate social questions. *But it was new on the English stage.*

Shaw had set his heart on writing plays, and he was not unduly worried about the frustrations and his apparent failures in his early plays, all specially written for leading actors and actresses of the London stage. His ideas were far ahead of their time, and so were his plays; so too, perhaps, were they beyond the understanding of the actors taking the parts in them. But he soon won through. Perhaps it was partly because people got to like his provocative manner – even if they disagreed with him politically. They certainly appreciated the wit and sparkling dialogue of which his plays are so full.

Shaw died in 1950 at the age of ninety-four. His was not only a very long life but a very productive one too. He was writing plays right up to the time of his death – he turned out fifty plays over a period of fifty years – though many would say that his greatest creative work was over when he wrote *The Apple Cart* in 1929 or even *Saint Joan* in 1923.

Although Shaw's reputation will stand principally on a handful of his long plays, his shorter pieces deserve greater attention than they have hitherto received. He wrote nearly twenty of these, mainly in the period 1904–1917, a period to which two of his shorter full-length plays, *Androcles and the Lion* and *Fanny's First Play*, belong. Shaw's thoughts were on social and political problems during much of this period, and it seems that he was merely 'keeping his hand in' with slighter pieces at the time. Nevertheless they are worth study *and they are worth staging*. They have the same characteristics as Shaw's longer plays: wit, inventiveness, versatility, propaganda (Shaw speaking through the mouths of his characters), a sense of 'theatre', and the obviously deliberate intention to outrage his audience. Two, at least, of them, *The Dark Lady of the Sonnets* and *The Shewing-up of Blanco Posnet*, are minor classics in their own right. Others echo some of the burning issues and world events of their day. All have something interesting and worthwhile to say. A place should be found for some of them in the dramatic repertoire of all secondary schools and places of further education.

Bramcote Hills,   JEFFERY TILLETT
Nottingham

How He Lied to Her Husband

Nothing in the theatre is staler than the situation of husband, wife, and lover, or the fun of knock-about farce. I have taken both, and got an original play out of them, as anybody else can if only he will look about him for his material instead of plagiarizing *Othello* and the thousand plays that have proceeded on Othello's romantic assumptions and false point of honour.

CHARACTERS

MR APJOHN, *the lover*
MR BOMPAS, *the husband*
AURORA BOMPAS, *the wife*

SCENE: A well-furnished flat in Kensington.

PERIOD: Early Edwardian.

The play was first produced simultaneously in London
and New York on 26 September 1904. In London the
parts of the lover, wife and husband were played by
Harley Granville-Barker, Gertrude Kingston and
A. G. Poulton; and in New York by Arnold Daly,
Selene Johnson and Dodson Mitchell.

HOW HE LIED TO HER HUSBAND

An account of the circumstances in which this play came to be written is not without interest. Shaw's ready inventiveness, wit, enterprise, sense of 'theatre', and speed of composition are all shown to advantage.

In 1895 Shaw wrote *The Man of Destiny*, a play in which the chief character is Napoleon Bonaparte. It was first produced in London in 1897. In 1904 it was to be produced for the first time in New York. Now *The Man of Destiny* is best described as a long-short play; its one long scene runs for about 70 minutes: 'too long to take a secondary place in the evening's performance, yet too short to suffice by itself'. The American producer Arnold Daly (who was playing the part of Napoleon) felt that a 'curtain-raiser' was needed to fill out the evening to about two hours' entertainment. Shaw obliged by turning out in a matter of days *How He Lied to Her Husband*; in Shaw's own words he 'took advantage of four days' continuous rain during a holiday in the north of Scotland' to write the play.

How He Lied to Her Husband is a farce, really little more than a revue sketch, on the husband–wife–lover theme. It is, in a way, Shaw's reaction to the oversentimental attitude of the playgoing public to his own play *Candida* which had been played in both London and New York in the previous year. By a neat arrangement – hardly a coincidence – *How He Lied* was given its first performance in both cities on the same day. The point Shaw was making could hardly be lost on his two audiences. But he made doubly sure that it was not by including references to *Candida* in his original version of the play. It is this version that I have used for this edition, with the original *Candida* references placed in parentheses; they can, if desired, be omitted at performances since later editions of the play are published without them.

The play is a delicious piece of fooling, very anti-romantic – as a contrast to the play it mocked at – and very far-fetched. It has some witty lines and a surprise ending that should bring gales of laughter at the fall of the curtain. But it needs lively acting and a good pace; everything must be overplayed and exaggerated.

In production the atmosphere of the Edwardian period – dress, setting, style – should be aimed at; though the editor has successfully produced the play in the manner of the 1930's.

HOW HE LIED TO HER HUSBAND

*It is eight o'clock in the evening. The curtains are drawn and the lamps
lighted in the drawing-room of Her flat in Cromwell Road. Her lover,
a beautiful youth of eighteen, in evening dress and cape, with a bunch of
flowers and an opera hat in his hands, comes in alone. The door is near
the corner; and as he appears in the doorway, he has the fireplace on
the nearest wall to his right, and the grand piano along the opposite
wall to his left. Near the fireplace a small ornamental table has on it
a hand mirror, a fan, a pair of long white gloves, and a little white
woollen cloud to wrap a woman's head in. On the other side of the room,
near the piano, is a broad, square, softly upholstered stool. The room
is furnished in the most approved South Kensington fashion: that is,
it is as like a show room as possible, and is intended to demonstrate the
social position and spending powers of its owners, and not in the least
to make them comfortable.*

*He is, be it repeated, a very beautiful youth, moving as in a dream,
walking as on air. He puts his flowers down carefully on the table
beside the fan; takes off his cape, and, as there is no room on the table
for it, takes it to the piano; puts his hat on the cape; crosses to the
hearth; looks at his watch; puts it up again; notices the things on the
table; lights up as if he saw heaven opening before him; goes to the
table and takes the cloud in both hands, nestling his nose into its softness
and kissing it; kisses the gloves one after another; kisses the fan;
gasps a long shuddering sigh of ecstasy; sits down on the stool and
presses his hands to his eyes to shut out reality and dream a little;
takes his hands down and shakes his head with a little smile of rebuke
for his folly; catches sight of a speck of dust on his shoes and hastily
and carefully brushes it off with his handkerchief; rises and takes the
hand mirror from the table to make sure of his tie with the gravest
anxiety; and is looking at his watch again when* SHE *comes in, much*

flustered. As she is dressed for the theatre; has spoilt, petted ways; and wears many diamonds, she has an air of being a young and beautiful woman; but as a matter of hard fact, she is, dress and pretentions apart, a very ordinary South Kensington female of about thirty-seven, hopelessly inferior in physical and spiritual distinction to the beautiful youth, who hastily puts down the mirror as she enters.

HE (*kissing her hand*): At last!

SHE: Henry: something dreadful has happened.

HE: What's the matter?

SHE: I have lost your poems.

HE: They were unworthy of you. I will write you some more.

SHE: No, thank you. Never any more poems for me. Oh, how could I have been so mad! so rash! so imprudent!

HE: Thank Heaven for your madness, your rashness, your imprudence!

SHE (*impatiently*): Oh, be sensible, Henry. Can't you see what a terrible thing this is for me? Suppose anybody finds these poems! what will they think?

HE: They will think that a man once loved a woman more devotedly than ever man loved woman before. But they will not know what man it was.

SHE: What good is that to me if everybody will know what woman it was?

HE: But how will they know?

SHE: How will they know! Why, my name is all over them: my silly, unhappy name. Oh, if I had only been christened Mary Jane, or Gladys Muriel, or Beatrice, or Francesca, or Guinevere, or something quite common! But Aurora! Aurora! I'm the only Aurora in London; and everybody knows it. I believe I'm the only Aurora in the world. And it's so horribly easy to rhyme to it! Oh, Henry, why didn't you try to restrain your feelings a little in common consideration for me? Why didn't you write with some little reserve?

HE: Write poems to you with reserve! You ask me that!

SHE (*with perfunctory tenderness*): Yes, dear, of course it was very

nice of you; and I know it was my own fault as much as yours.
I ought to have noticed that your verses ought never to have
been addressed to a married woman.

HE: Ah, how I wish they had been addressed to an unmarried
woman! how I wish they had!

SHE: Indeed you have no right to wish anything of the sort.
They are quite unfit for anybody but a married woman. That's
just the difficulty. What will my sisters-in-law think of them?

HE (*painfully jarred*): Have you got sisters-in-law?

SHE: Yes, of course I have. Do you suppose I am an angel?

HE (*biting his lips*): I do. Heaven help me, I do – or I did – or
(HE *almost chokes a sob*).

SHE (*softening and putting her hand caressingly on his shoulder*): Listen
to me, dear. It's very nice of you to live with me in a dream,
and to love me, and so on; but I can't help my husband having
disagreeable relatives, can I?

HE (*brightening up*): Ah, of course they are your husband's
relatives: I forgot that. Forgive me, Aurora. (HE *takes her hand
from his shoulder and kisses it.* SHE *sits down on the stool.* HE *remains
near the table, with his back to it, smiling fatuously down at her.*)

SHE: The fact is, Teddy's got nothing but relatives. He has
eight sisters and six half-sisters, and ever so many brothers –
but I don't mind his brothers. Now if you only knew the
least little thing about the world, Henry, you'd know that in
a large family, though the sisters quarrel with one another like
mad all the time, yet let one of the brothers marry, and they
all turn on their unfortunate sister-in-law and devote the rest
of their lives with perfect unanimity to persuading him that
his wife is unworthy of him. They can do it to her very face
without her knowing it, because there are always a lot of
stupid low family jokes that nobody understands but themselves. Half the time you can't tell what they're talking about:
it just drives you wild. There ought to be a law against a
man's sister ever entering his house after he's married. I'm
as certain as that I'm sitting here that Georgina stole those
poems out of my workbox.

HE: She will not understand them, I think.

SHE: Oh, won't she! She'll understand them only too well. She'll understand more harm than ever was in them: nasty vulgar-minded cat!

HE (*going to her*): Oh don't, don't think of people in that way. Don't think of her at all. (HE *takes her hand and sits down on the carpet at her feet.*) Aurora: do you remember the evening when I sat here at your feet and read you those poems for the first time?

SHE: I shouldn't have let you: I see that now. When I think of Georgina sitting there at Teddy's feet and reading them to him for the first time, I feel I shall just go distracted.

HE: Yes, you are right. It will be a profanation.

SHE: Oh, I don't care about the profanation; but what will Teddy think? what will he do? (*Suddenly throwing his head away from her knee.*) You don't seem to think a bit about Teddy. (SHE *jumps up, more and more agitated.*)

HE (*supine on the floor; for she has thrown him off his balance*): To me Teddy is nothing, and Georgina less than nothing.

SHE: You'll soon find out how much less than nothing she is. If you think a woman can't do any harm because she's only a scandalmongering dowdy ragbag, you're greatly mistaken. (SHE *flounces about the room.* HE *gets up slowly and dusts his hands. Suddenly* SHE *runs to him and throws herself into his arms.*) Henry: help me. Find a way out of this for me; and I'll bless you as long as you live. Oh, how wretched I am! (SHE *sobs on his breast.*)

HE: And oh! how happy I am!

SHE (*whisking herself abruptly away*): Don't be selfish.

HE (*humbly*): Yes: I deserve that. I think if I were going to the stake with you, I should still be so happy with you that I could hardly feel your danger more than my own.

SHE (*relenting and patting his hand fondly*): Oh, you are a dear darling boy, Henry; but (*Throwing his hand away fretfully*) you're no use. I want somebody to tell me what to do.

HE (*with quiet conviction*): Your heart will tell you at the right

time. I have thought deeply over this; and I know what we
two must do, sooner or later.

SHE: No, Henry. I will do nothing improper, nothing dishonour-
able. (SHE *sits down plump on the stool and looks inflexible.*)

HE: If you did, you would no longer be Aurora. Our course is
perfectly simple, perfectly straightforward, perfectly stainless
and true. We love one another. I am not ashamed of that: I am
ready to go out and proclaim it to all London as simply as I
will declare it to your husband when you see – as you soon will
see – that this is the only way honourable enough for your
feet to tread. Let us go out together to our own house, this
evening, without concealment and without shame. Remember!
we owe something to your husband. We are his guests here:
he is an honourable man: he has been kind to us: he has perhaps
loved you as well as his prosaic nature and his sordid commercial environment permitted. We owe it to him in all
honour not to let him learn the truth from the lips of a scandal-
monger. Let us go to him now quietly, hand in hand; bid him
farewell; and walk out of the house without concealment and
subterfuge, freely and honestly, in full honour and self-respect.

SHE (*staring at him*): And where shall we go to?

HE: We shall not depart by a hair's breadth from the ordinary
natural current of our lives. We were going to the theatre
when the loss of the poems compelled us to take action at
once. We shall go to the theatre still; but we shall leave your
diamonds here; for we cannot afford diamonds, and do not
need them.

SHE (*fretfully*): I have told you already that I hate diamonds;
only Teddy insists on hanging me all over with them. You
need not preach simplicity to me.

HE: I never thought of doing so, dearest: I know that these
trivialities are nothing to you. What was I saying? – oh yes.
Instead of coming back here from the theatre, you will come
with me to my home – now and henceforth our home – and in
due course of time, when you are divorced, we shall go
through whatever idle legal ceremony you may desire. *I*

attach no importance to the law: my love was not created in me by the law, nor can it be bound or loosed by it. That is simple enough, and sweet enough, is it not? (HE *takes the flowers from the table*.) Here are flowers for you: I have the tickets: we will ask your husband to lend us the carriage to show that there is no malice, no grudge, between us. Come!

SHE (*spiritlessly, taking the flowers without looking at them, and temporizing*): Teddy isn't in yet.

HE: Well, let us take that calmly. Let us go to the theatre as if nothing had happened, and tell him when we come back. Now or three hours hence: today or tomorrow: what does it matter, provided all is done in honour, without shame or fear?

[SHE: What did you get tickets for? Lohengrin?

HE: I tried; but Lohengrin was sold out for tonight. (HE *takes out two Court Theatre tickets*.)

SHE: Then what did you get?

HE: Can you ask me? What is there besides Lohengrin that we two could endure, except Candida?

SHE (*springing up*): Candida! No, I won't go to it again, Henry (*Tossing the flowers on the piano*). It is that play that has done all the mischief. I'm very sorry I ever saw it: it ought to be stopped.

HE (*amazed*): Aurora!

SHE: Yes: I mean it.

HE: That divinest love poem! the poem that gave us courage to speak to one another! that revealed to us what we really felt for one another! that —

SHE: Just so. It put a lot of stuff into my head that I should never have dreamt of for myself. I imagined myself just like Candida.

HE (*catching her hands and looking earnestly at her*): You were right. You are like Candida.

SHE (*snatching her hands away*): Oh, stuff! And I thought you were just like Eugene. (*Looking critically at him.*) Now that I come to look at you, you are rather like him, too. (SHE *throws herself discontentedly into the nearest seat, which happens to be the bench at the piano.* HE *goes to her.*)

HE (*very earnestly*): Aurora: if Candida had loved Eugene she would have gone out into the night with him without a moment's hesitation.

SHE (*with equal earnestness*): Henry: do you know what's wanting in that play?

HE: There is nothing wanting in it.

SHE: Yes there is. There's a Georgina wanting in it. If Georgina had been there to make trouble, that play would have been a true-to-life tragedy. Now I'll tell you something about it that I have never told you before.

HE: What is that?

SHE: I took Teddy to it. I thought it would do him good; and so it would if I could only have kept him awake. Georgina came too; and you should have heard the way she went on about it. She said it was downright immoral, and that she knew the sort of woman that encourages boys to sit on the hearthrug and make love to her. She was just preparing Teddy's mind to poison it about me.

HE: Let us be just to Georgina, dearest —

SHE: Let her deserve it first. Just to Georgina, indeed!

HE: She really sees the world in that way. That is her punishment.

SHE: How can it be her punishment when she likes it? It'll be my punishment when she brings that budget of poems to Teddy. I wish you'd have some sense, and sympathize with my position a little.

HE (*going away from the piano and beginning to walk about rather testily*): My dear: I really don't care about Georgina or about Teddy. All these squabbles belong to a plane on which I am, as you say, no use. I have counted the cost; and I do not fear the consequences. After all, what is there to fear? Where is the difficulty? What can Georgina do? What can your husband do? What can anybody do?]

SHE: Do you mean to say that you propose that we should

walk right bang up to Teddy and tell him we're going away together?

HE: Yes. What can be simpler?

SHE: And do you think for a moment he'd stand it [like that half-baked clergyman in the play]? He'd just kill you.

HE (*coming to a sudden stop and speaking with considerable confidence*): You don't understand these things, my darling: how could you? [In one respect I am unlike the poet in the play.] I have followed the Greek ideal and not neglected the culture of my body. I have a passion for pugilism. Your husband would make a tolerable second-rate heavyweight if he were in training and ten years younger. As it is, he could, if strung up to a great effort by a burst of passion, give a good account of himself for perhaps fifteen seconds. But I am active enough to keep out of his reach for fifteen seconds; and after that I should be simply all over him.

SHE (*rising and coming to him in consternation*): What do you mean by all over him?

HE (*gently*): Don't ask me, dearest. At all events, I swear to you that you need not be anxious about me.

SHE: And what about Teddy? Do you mean to tell me that you are going to beat Teddy before my face like a brutal prize-fighter?

HE: All this alarm is needless, dearest. Believe me, nothing will happen. Your husband knows that I am capable of defending myself. Under such circumstances nothing ever does happen. And of course *I* shall do nothing. The man who once loved you is sacred to me.

SHE (*suspiciously*): Doesn't he love me still? Has he told you anything?

HE: No, no. (HE *takes her tenderly in his arms.*) Dearest, dearest: how agitated you are! how unlike yourself! All these worries belong to the lower plane. Come up with me to the higher one. The heights, the solitudes, the soul world!

SHE (*avoiding his gaze*): No: stop: it's no use, Mr Apjohn.

HE (*recoiling*): Mr Apjohn!!!

SHE: Excuse me: I mean Henry, of course.

HE: How could you even think of me as Mr Apjohn? I never think of you as Mrs Bompas: it is always Cand – I mean Aurora, Aurora, Auro —

SHE: Yes, yes: that's all very well, Mr Apjohn (*He is about to interrupt again: but she won't have it.*) no: it's no use: I've suddenly begun to think of you as Mr Apjohn; and it's ridiculous to go on calling you Henry. I thought you were only a boy, a child, a dreamer. I thought you would be too much afraid to do anything. And now you want to beat Teddy and to break up my home and disgrace me and make a horrible scandal in the papers. It's cruel, unmanly, cowardly.

HE (*with grave wonder*): Are you afraid?

SHE: Oh, of course I'm afraid. So would you be if you had any common sense. (SHE *goes to the hearth, turning her back to him, and puts one tapping foot on the fender.*)

HE (*watching her with great gravity*): Perfect love casteth out fear. That is why I am not afraid. Mrs Bompas: you do not love me.

SHE (*turning to him with a gasp of relief*): Oh, thank you, thank you! You really can be very nice, Henry.

HE: Why do you thank me?

SHE (*coming prettily to him from the fireplace*): For calling me Mrs Bompas again. I feel now that you are going to be reasonable and behave like a gentleman. (HE *drops on the stool; covers his face with his hands; and groans.*) What's the matter?

HE: Once or twice in my life I have dreamed that I was exquisitely happy and blessed. But oh! the misgiving at the first stir of consciousness! the stab of reality! the prison walls of the bedroom! the bitter, bitter disappointment of waking! And this time! oh, this time I thought I was awake.

SHE: Listen to me, Henry: we really haven't time for all that sort of flapdoodle now. (HE *starts to his feet as if she had pulled a trigger and straightened him by the release of a powerful spring, and goes past her with set teeth to the little table.*) Oh, take care: you nearly hit me in the chin with the top of your head.

HE (*with fierce politeness*): I beg your pardon. What is it you want

me to do? I am at your service. I am ready to behave like a
gentleman if you will be kind enough to explain exactly how.

SHE (*a little frightened*): Thank you, Henry: I was sure you would.
You're not angry with me, are you?

HE: Go on. Go on quickly. Give me something to think about,
or I will – I will —— (HE *suddenly snatches up her fan and is about to
break it in his clenched fists.*)

SHE (*running forward and catching at the fan, with loud lamentation*):
Don't break my fan – no, don't. (HE *slowly relaxes his grip of it
as she draws it anxiously out of his hands.*) No, really, that's a
stupid trick. I don't like that. You've no right to do that.
(SHE *opens the fan, and finds that the sticks are disconnected.*) Oh,
how could you be so inconsiderate?

HE: I beg your pardon. I will buy you a new one.

SHE (*querrulously*): You will never be able to match it. And it was
a particular favourite of mine.

HE (*shortly*): Then you will have to do without it: that's all.

SHE: That's not a very nice thing to say after breaking my pet
fan, I think.

HE: If you knew how near I was to breaking Teddy's pet wife
and presenting him with the pieces, you would be thankful
that you are alive instead of – of – of howling about five-
shillingsworth of ivory. Damn your fan!

SHE: Oh! Don't you dare swear in my presence. One would
think you were my husband.

HE (*again collapsing on the stool*): This is some horrible dream.
What has become of you? You are not my Aurora.

SHE: Oh, well, if you come to that, what has become of you?
Do you think I would ever have encouraged you if I had
known you were such a little devil?

HE: Don't drag me down – don't – don't. Help me to find the
way back to the heights.

SHE (*kneeling beside him and pleading*): If you would only be
reasonable, Henry. If you would only remember that I am on
the brink of ruin, and not go on calmly saying it's all quite
simple.

HE: It seems so to me.

SHE (*jumping up distractedly*): If you say that again I shall do something I'll be sorry for. Here we are, standing on the edge of a frightful precipice. No doubt it's quite simple to go over and have done with it. But can't you suggest anything more agreeable?

HE: I can suggest nothing now. A chill black darkness has fallen: I can see nothing but the ruins of our dream. (HE *rises with a deep sigh.*)

SHE: Can't you? Well, I can. I can see Georgina rubbing those poems into Teddy. (*Facing him determinedly.*) And I tell you, Henry Apjohn, that you got me into this mess; and you must get me out of it again.

HE (*polite but hopeless*): All I can say is that I am entirely at your service. What do you wish me to do?

SHE: Do you know anybody else named Aurora?

HE: No.

SHE: There's no use in saying No in that frozen pigheaded way. You must know some Aurora or other somewhere.

HE: You said you were the only Aurora in the world. And (*Lifting his clasped fists with a sudden return of his emotion.*) oh God! you were the only Aurora in the world to me. (HE *turns away from her, hiding his face.*)

SHE (*petting him*): Yes, yes, dear: of course. It's very nice of you; and I appreciate it: indeed I do; but it's not seasonable just at present. Now just listen to me. I suppose you know all those poems by heart.

HE: Yes, by heart. (*Raising his head and looking at her with a sudden suspicion.*) Don't you?

SHE: Well, I never can remember verses; and besides, I've been so busy that I've not had time to read them all; though I intend to the very first moment I can get: I promise you that most faithfully, Henry. But now try and remember very particularly. Does the name of Bompas occur in any of the poems?

HE (*indignantly*): No.

SHE: You're quite sure?

HE: Of course I am quite sure. How could I use such a name in a poem?

SHE: Well, I don't see why not. It rhymes to rumpus, which seems appropriate enough at present, goodness knows! However, you're a poet, and you ought to know.

HE: What does it matter – now?

SHE: It matters a lot, I can tell you. If there's nothing about Bompas in the poems, we can say that they were written to some other Aurora, and that you showed them to me because my name was Aurora too. So you've got to invent another Aurora for the occasion.

HE (*very coldly*): Oh, if you wish me to tell a lie —

SHE: Surely, as a man of honour – as a gentleman, you wouldn't tell the truth, would you?

HE: Very well. You have broken my spirit and desecrated my dreams. I will lie and protest and stand on my honour: oh, I will play the gentleman, never fear.

SHE: Yes, put it all on me, of course. Don't be mean, Henry.

HE (*rousing himself with an effort*): You are quite right, Mrs Bompas: I beg your pardon. You must excuse my temper. I have got growing pains, I think.

SHE: Growing pains!

HE: The process of growing from romantic boyhood into cynical maturity usually takes fifteen years. When it is compressed into fifteen minutes, the pace is too fast; and growing pains are the result.

SHE: Oh, is this a time for cleverness? It's settled, isn't it, that you're going to be nice and good, and that you'll brazen it out to Teddy that you have some other Aurora?

HE: Yes: I'm capable of anything now. I should not have told him the truth by halves; and now I will not lie by halves. I'll wallow in the honour of a gentleman.

SHE: Dearest boy, I knew you would. I — Sh! (SHE *rushes to the door, and holds it ajar, listening breathlessly.*)

HE: What is it?

SHE (*white with apprehension*): It's Teddy: I hear him tapping the new barometer. He can't have anything serious on his mind or he wouldn't do that. Perhaps Georgina hasn't said anything. (SHE *steals back to the hearth.*) Try and look as if there was nothing the matter. Give me my gloves, quick. (HE *hands them to her.* SHE *pulls on one hastily and begins buttoning it with ostentatious unconcern.*) Go farther away from me, quick. (HE *walks doggedly away from her until the piano prevents his going farther.*) If I button my glove, and you were to hum a tune, don't you think that —

HE: The tableau would be complete in its guiltiness. For Heaven's sake, Mrs Bompas, let that glove alone: you look like a pickpocket.

Her husband comes in: a robust, thicknecked, well-groomed city man, with a strong chin but a blithering eye and credulous mouth. HE *has a momentous air, but shows no sign of displeasure: rather the contrary.*

HER HUSBAND: Hallo! I thought you two were at the theatre.

SHE: I felt anxious about you, Teddy. Why didn't you come home to dinner?

HER HUSBAND: I got a message from Georgina. She wanted me to go to her.

SHE: Poor dear Georgina! I'm sorry I haven't been able to call on her this last week. I hope there's nothing the matter with her.

HER HUSBAND: Nothing, except anxiety for my welfare – and yours. (SHE *steals a terrified look at Henry.*) By the way, Apjohn, I should like a word with you this evening, if Aurora can spare you for a moment.

HE (*formally*): I am at your service.

HER HUSBAND: No hurry. After the theatre will do.

HE: We have decided not to go.

HER HUSBAND: Indeed! Well, then, shall we adjourn to my snuggery?

SHE: You needn't move. I shall go and lock up my diamonds since I'm not going to the theatre. Give me my things.

HER HUSBAND (*as he hands her the cloud and the mirror*): Well, we shall have more room here.

HE (*looking about him and shaking his shoulders loose*): I think I should prefer plenty of room.

HER HUSBAND: So, if it's not disturbing you, Rory —?

SHE: Not at all. (SHE *goes out.*)

When the two men are along together, BOMPAS *deliberately takes the poems from his breast pocket; looks at them reflectively; then looks at Henry, mutely inviting his attention.* HENRY *refuses to understand, doing his best to look unconcerned.*

HER HUSBAND: Do these manuscripts seem at all familiar to you, may I ask?

HE: Manuscripts?

HER HUSBAND: Yes. Would you like to look at them a little closer? (*He proffers them under Henry's nose.*)

HE (*as with a sudden illumination of glad surprise*): Why, these are my poems!

HER HUSBAND: So I gather.

HE: What a shame! Mrs Bompas has shown them to you! You must think me an utter ass. I wrote them years ago after reading Swinburne's 'Songs Before Sunrise'. Nothing would do me then but I must reel off a set of Songs to the Sunrise. Aurora, you know: the rosy-fingered Aurora. They're all about Aurora. When Mrs Bompas told me her name was Aurora, I couldn't resist the temptation to lend them to her to read. But I didn't bargain for your unsympathetic eyes.

HER HUSBAND (*grinning*): Apjohn: that's really very ready of you. You are cut out for literature; and the day will come when Rory and I will be proud to have you about the house. I have heard far thinner stories from much older men.

HE (*with an air of great surprise*): Do you mean to imply that you don't believe me?

HER HUSBAND: Do you expect me to believe you?

HE: Why not? I don't understand.

HER HUSBAND: Come! Don't underrate your own cleverness, Apjohn. I think you understand pretty well.

HE: I assure you I am quite at a loss. Can you not be a little more explicit?

HER HUSBAND: Don't overdo it, old chap. However, I will just be so far explicit as to say that if you think these poems read as if they were addressed, not to a live woman, but to a shivering cold time of day at which you were never out of bed in your life, you hardly do justice to your own literary powers – which I admire and appreciate, mind you, as much as any man. Come! own up. You wrote those poems to my wife. (*An internal struggle prevents Henry from answering.*) Of course you did. (*He throws the poems on the table; and goes to the hearthrug, where he plants himself solidly, chuckling a little and waiting for the next move.*)

HE (*formally and carefully*): Mr Bompas: I pledge you my word you are mistaken. I need not tell you that Mrs Bompas is a lady of stainless honour, who has never cast an unworthy thought on me. The fact that she has shown you my poems —

HER HUSBAND: That's not a fact. I came by them without her knowledge. She didn't show them to me.

HE: Does not that prove their perfect innocence? She would have shown them to you at once if she had taken your quite unfounded view on them.

HER HUSBAND (*shaken*): Apjohn: play fair. Don't abuse your intellectual gifts. Do you really mean that I am making a fool of myself?

HE (*earnestly*): Believe me, you are. I assure you, on my honour as a gentleman, that I have never had the slightest feeling for Mrs Bompas beyond the ordinary esteem and regard of a pleasant acquaintance.

HER HUSBAND (*shortly, showing ill humour for the first time*): Oh, indeed. (*He leaves his hearth and begins to approach Henry slowly, looking him up and down with growing resentment.*)

HE (*hastening to improve the impression made by his mendacity*): I should never have dreamt of writing poems to her. The thing is absurd.

HER HUSBAND (*reddening ominously*): Why is it absurd?

HE (*shrugging his shoulders*): Well, it happens that I do not admire Mrs Bompas – in that way.

HER HUSBAND (*breaking out in Henry's face*): Let me tell you that Mrs Bompas has been admired by better men than you, you soapy-headed little puppy, you.

HE (*much taken aback*): There is no need to insult me like this. I assure you, on my honour as a —

HER HUSBAND (*too angry to tolerate a reply, and boring Henry more and more towards the piano*): You don't admire Mrs Bompas! You would never dream of writing poems to Mrs Bompas! My wife's not good enough for you, isn't she? (*Fiercely.*) Who are you, pray, that you should be so jolly superior?

HE: Mr Bompas: I can make allowances for your jealousy —

HER HUSBAND: Jealousy! do you suppose I'm jealous of you? No, nor of ten like you. But if you think I'll stand here and let you insult my wife in her own house, you're mistaken.

HE (*very uncomfortable with his back against the piano and TEDDY standing over him threateningly*): How can I convince you? Be reasonable. I tell you my relations with Mrs Bompas are relations of perfect coldness – of indifference —

HER HUSBAND (*scornfully*): Say it again: say it again. You're proud of it, aren't you? Yah! you're not worth kicking.

HENRY *suddenly executes the feat known to pugilists as slipping, and changes sides with Teddy, who is now between Henry and the piano.*

HE: Look here: I'm not going to stand this.

HER HUSBAND: Oh, you have some blood in your body after all! Good job!

HE: This is ridiculous. I assure you Mrs Bompas is quite —

HER HUSBAND: What is Mrs Bompas to you, I'd like to know. I'll tell you what Mrs Bompas is. She's the smartest woman in the smartest set in South Kensington, and the handsomest, and the cleverest, and the most fetching to experienced men who know a good thing when they see it, whatever she may be to conceited penny-a-lining puppies who think nothing good enough for them. It's admitted by the best people; and not to know it argues yourself unknown. Three of our first actor-managers have offered her a hundred a week if she'll go on the stage when they start a repertory theatre; and I think they know what they're about as well as you. The only member of the present Cabinet that you might call a handsome man has neglected the business of the country to dance with her, though he don't belong to our set as a regular thing. One of the first professional poets in Bedford Park wrote a sonnet to her, worth all your amateur trash. At Ascot last season the eldest son of a duke excused himself from calling on me on the ground that his feelings for Mrs Bompas were not consistent with his duty to me as host; and it did him honour and me too. But (*With gathering fury*) she isn't good enough for you, it seems. You regard her with coldness, with indifference; and you have the cool cheek to tell me so to my face. For two pins I'd flatten your nose in to teach you manners. Introducing a fine woman to you is casting pearls before swine (*Yelling at him*) before SWINE! d'ye hear?

HE (*with a deplorable lack of polish*): You call me a swine again and I'll land you one on the chin that'll make your head sing for a week.

HER HUSBAND (*exploding*): What —!

He charges at Henry with bull-like fury. HENRY *places himself on guard in the manner of a well-taught boxer, and gets away smartly, but unfortunately forgets the stool which is just behind him. He falls backwards over it, unintentionally pushing it against the shins of* BOMPAS, *who falls forward over it.* MRS BOMPAS, *with a scream, rushes into the room between the sprawling champions, and sits down on the floor in order to get her right arm round her husband's neck.*

SHE: You shan't, Teddy: you shan't. You will be killed: he is a prizefighter.

HER HUSBAND (*vengefully*): I'll prizefight him. (*He struggles vainly to free himself from her embrace.*)

SHE: Henry: don't let him fight you. Promise me that you won't.

HE (*ruefully*): I have got a most frightful bump on the back of my head. (HE *tries to rise.*)

SHE (*reaching out her left hand to seize his coat tail, and pulling him*

down again, whilst keeping fast hold of Teddy with the other hand):
Not until you have promised: not until you both have promised. (TEDDY *tries to rise: she pulls him back again.*) Teddy:
you promise, don't you? Yes, yes. Be good: you promise.

HER HUSBAND: I won't, unless he takes it back.

SHE: He will: he does. You take it back, Henry? – yes.

HE (*savagely*): Yes. I take it back. (SHE *lets go his coat.* HE *gets up.
So does* TEDDY.) I take it all back, all, without reserve.

SHE (*on the carpet*): Is nobody going to help me up? (*They each
take a hand and pull her up.*) Now won't you shake hands and
be good?

HE (*recklessly*): I shall do nothing of the sort. I have steeped
myself in lies for your sake; and the only reward I get is a
lump on the back of my head the size of an apple. Now I will
go back to the straight path.

SHE: Henry: for Heaven's sake —

HE: It's no use. Your husband is a fool and a brute —

HER HUSBAND: What's that you say?

HE: I say you are a fool and a brute; and if you'll step outside
with me I'll say it again. (TEDDY *begins to take off his coat for
combat.*) Those poems were written to your wife, every word
of them, and to nobody else. (*The scowl clears away from Bompas's
countenance. Radiant, he replaces his coat.*) I wrote them because
I loved her. I thought her the most beautiful woman in the
world; and I told her so over and over again. I adored her: do
you hear? I told her that you were a sordid commercial chump,
utterly unworthy of her; and so you are.

HER HUSBAND (*so gratified, he can hardly believe his ears*): You
don't mean it!

HE: Yes, I do mean it, and a lot more too. I asked Mrs Bompas
to walk out of the house with me – to leave you – to get
divorced from you and marry me. I begged and implored
her to do it this very night. It was her refusal that ended everything between us. (*Looking very disparagingly at him.*) What she
can see in you, goodness only knows!

HER HUSBAND (*beaming with remorse*): My dear chap, why

didn't you say so before? I apologize. Come! don't bear malice: shake hands. Make him shake hands, Rory.

SHE: For my sake, Henry. After all, he's my husband. Forgive him. Take his hand. (HENRY, *dazed, lets her take his hand and place it in Teddy's.*)

HER HUSBAND (*shaking it heartily*): You've got to own that none of your literary heroines can touch my Rory. (*He turns to her and claps her with fond pride on the shoulder.*) Eh, Rory? They can't resist you: none of 'em. Never knew a man yet that could hold out three days.

SHE: Don't be foolish, Teddy. I hope you were not really hurt, Henry. (SHE *feels the back of his head.* HE *flinches.*) Oh, poor boy, what a bump! I must get some vinegar and brown paper. (SHE *goes to the bell and rings.*)

HER HUSBAND: Will you do me a great favour, Apjohn. I hardly like to ask; but it would be a real kindness to us both.

HE: What can I do?

HER HUSBAND (*taking up the poems*): Well, may I get these printed? It shall be done in the best style. The finest paper, sumptuous binding, everything first class. They're beautiful poems. I should like to show them about a bit.

SHE (*running back from the bell, delighted with the idea, and coming between them*): Oh Henry, if you wouldn't mind!

HE: Oh, *I* don't mind. I am past minding anything. I have grown too fast this evening.

SHE: How old are you, Henry?

HE: This morning I was eighteen. Now I am – confound it! I'm quoting that beast of a play. (HE *takes the Candida tickets out of his pocket and tears them up viciously.*)

HER HUSBAND: What shall we call the volume? To Aurora, or something like that, eh?

HE: I should call it How He Lied to Her Husband.

Passion, Poison, and Petrifaction

or, THE FATAL GAZOGENE

A Brief Tragedy for Barns and Booths

All playwrights and all actors tomfool sometimes if they
can. The practice needs no apology if it amuses them and
their audiences harmlessly. Irresponsible laughter is
salutary in small quantities.

CHARACTERS

LADY MAGNESIA FITZTOLLEMACHE
SIR GEORGE FITZTOLLEMACHE, *her husband*
ADOLPHUS BASTABLE, *her lover*
PHYLLIS, *her maid*
THE LANDLORD (or LANDLADY)
A POLICEMAN
A DOCTOR

SCENE: A bed-sitting-room, South Kensington. Late at night.

This play was first performed in a booth in Regent's Park on 14 July 1905 for the benefit of the Actors' Orphanage.

PASSION, POISON, AND PETRIFACTION;
OR, THE FATAL GAZOGENE*

Passion, Poison, and Petrifaction, which Shaw called 'a brief tragedy for barns and booths', is, like *The Dark Lady of the Sonnets* and *How He Lied to Her Husband*, a play written for a special purpose. In this case we have Shaw meeting a request by writing a short piece of nonsense in aid of a worthy cause – the funds of the Actors' Orphanage. Shaw was extremely fond of children. (It was with audiences of young people in mind that he wrote *Androcles and the Lion*.) On one occasion he told an impromptu story to the young childen of a friend; in this story a cat lapped up a saucer of moist plaster of paris and was petrified. This was the origin of his ludicrously funny little play, *Passion, Poison and Petrifaction*.

The play was originally performed in a booth erected in Regent's Park in the summer of 1905. It had a star-studded cast. Among those taking part were Irene Vanbrugh, Nancy Price, and Cyril Maude. It was immensely successful and was given several repeat performances.

Like *How He Lied to Her Husband*, written in the previous year, it is based on the eternal triangle theme – husband, wife and lover – but treated in a highly farcical fashion. Here Shaw's fooling is at its most absurd.

Some producers fight shy of this little play. Perhaps they feel that the equally absurd effects that Shaw calls for are quite impossible. To take this view is to miss the point that half the fun in performing it is in the hilarious manner in which those same 'difficulties' are overcome. It is a piece of 'tomfoolery' – as Shaw himself called it – and an audience will be indulgent and forgive makeshift effects, however fantastic and far-fetched. For instance,

*A Soda-water Syphon with a device for producing its own soda-water.

Shaw himself suggested sugar icing (as used on wedding cakes) in place of plaster. 'There is but little difference between the two substances; but the taste of the wedding cake is considered more agreeable by many people.'

An impromptu 'orchestra' can be used if this will 'enhance the effect'. (Shaw stipulated a harp, a drum and a pair of cymbals! Anything will do: mouth-organ, comb-and-tissue, guitar . . .) The part of the Landlord can be taken by a woman (as a Land-lady); and the 'Bill Bailey' song can be dropped in favour of anything in the current 'Top Twenty' charts. Shaw sanctioned both these substitutions in an introductory note to the play.

Have a go at it! But do remember how important timing is in a piece of this nature.

PASSION, POISON, AND PETRIFACTION

---

*In a bed-sitting-room in a fashionable quarter of London a lady sits at
her dressing-table, with her maid combing her hair. It is late; and
the electric lamps are glowing. Apparently the room is bedless; but
there stands against the opposite wall to that at which the dressing-
table is placed a piece of furniture that suggests a bookcase without
carrying conviction. On the same side is a chest of drawers of that
disastrous kind which, recalcitrant to the opener until she is provoked
to violence, then suddenly come wholly out and defy all her efforts to
fit them in again. Opposite this chest of drawers, on the lady's side of
the room, is a cupboard. The presence of a row of gentleman's boots
beside the chest of drawers proclaims that the lady is married. Her
own boots are beside the cupboard. The third wall is pierced midway
by the door, above which is a cuckoo clock. Near the door a pedestal
bears a portrait bust of the lady in plaster. There is a fan on the
dressing-table, a hatbox and rug strap on the chest of drawers, an
umbrella and a bootjack against the wall near the bed. The general
impression is one of brightness, beauty, and social ambition, damped
by somewhat inadequate means. A certain air of theatricality is
produced by the fact that though the room is rectangular it has only
three walls. Not a sound is heard except the overture and the crackling
of the lady's hair as the maid's brush draws electric sparks from it in
the dry air of the London midsummer.*
The cuckoo clock strikes sixteen.

THE LADY: How much did the clock strike, Phyllis?
PHYLLIS: Sixteen, my lady.
THE LADY: That means eleven o'clock, does it not?
PHYLLIS: Eleven at night, my lady. In the morning it means

half past two; so if you hear it strike sixteen during your slumbers, do not rise.

THE LADY: I will not, Phyllis. Phyllis: I am weary. I will go to bed. Prepare my couch.

PHYLLIS *crosses the room to the bookcase and touches a button. The front of the bookcase falls out with a crash and becomes a bed. A roll of distant thunder echoes the crash.*

PHYLLIS (*shuddering*): It is a terrible night. Heaven help all poor mariners at sea! My master is late. I trust nothing has happened to him. Your bed is ready, my lady.

THE LADY: Thank you, Phyllis. (*She rises and approaches the bed.*) Goodnight.

PHYLLIS: Will your ladyship not undress?

THE LADY: Not tonight, Phyllis. (*Glancing through where the fourth wall is missing.*) Not under the circumstances.

PHYLLIS (*impulsively throwing herself on her knees by her mistress's side, and clasping her round the waist*): Oh, my beloved mistress, I know not why or how; but I feel that I shall never see you alive again. There is murder in the air. (*Thunder.*) Hark!

THE LADY: Strange! As I sat there methought I heard angels singing, Oh, won't you come home, Bill Bailey? Why should angels call me Bill Bailey? My name is Magnesia Fitztollemache.

PHYLLIS (*emphasizing the title*): Lady Magnesia Fitztollemache.

LADY MAGNESIA: In case we should never again meet in this world, let us take a last farewell.

PHYLLIS (*embracing her with tears*): My poor murdered angel mistress!

LADY MAGNESIA: In case we should meet again, call me at half past eleven.

PHYLLIS: I will, I will.

PHYLLIS *withdraws, overcome by emotion.* LADY MAGNESIA *switches off the electric light, and immediately hears the angels quite distinctly. They sing* Bill Bailey *so sweetly that she can attend to nothing else, and forgets to remove even her boots as she draws the coverlet over herself and sinks to sleep, lulled by celestial harmony. A*

*white radiance plays on her pillow, and lights up her beautiful face.
But the thunder growls again; and a lurid red glow concentrates itself
on the door, which is presently flung open, revealing a saturnine figure in
evening dress, partially concealed by a crimson cloak. As he steals
towards the bed the unnatural glare in his eyes and the broad-bladed
dagger nervously gripped in his right hand bode ill for the sleeping lady.
Providentially she sneezes on the very brink of eternity; and the tension
of the murderer's nerves is such that he bolts precipitately under the
bed at the sudden and startling* Atscha! *A dull, heavy, rhythmic
thumping – the beating of his heart – betrays his whereabouts. Soon he
emerges cautiously and raises his head above the bed coverlet level.*

THE MURDERER: I can no longer cower here listening to the
agonized thumpings of my own heart. She but snooze in her
sleep. I'll do't. (*He again raises the dagger. The angels sing again.
He cowers.*) What is this? Has the tune reached Heaven?

LADY MAGNESIA (*waking and sitting up*): My husband! (*All the
colours of the rainbow chase one another up his face with ghastly
brilliancy.*) Why do you change colour? And what on earth are
you doing with that dagger?

FITZ (*affecting unconcern, but unhinged*): It is a present for you: a
present from mother. Pretty, isn't it? (*He displays it fatuously.*)

LADY MAGNESIA: But she promised me a fish slice.

FITZ: This is a combination fish slice and dagger. One day you
have salmon for dinner. The next you have a murder to commit. See?

LADY MAGNESIA: My sweet mother-in-law! (*Someone knocks at
the door.*) That is Adolphus's knock. (FITZ'S *face turns a dazzling
green.*) What has happened to your complexion? You have
turned green. Now I think of it, you always do when Adolphus
is mentioned. Arn't you going to let him in?

FITZ: Certainly not. (*He goes to the door.*) Adolphus: you cannot
enter. My wife is undressed and in bed.

LADY MAGNESIA (*rising*): I am not. Come in, Adolphus. (*She
switches on the electric light.*)

ADOLPHUS (*without*): Something most important has happened.
I must come in for a moment.

FITZ (*calling to Adolphus*): Something important happened? What is it?

ADOLPHUS (*without*): My new clothes have come home.

FITZ: He says his new clothes have come home.

LADY MAGNESIA (*running to the door and opening it*): Oh, come in, come in. Let me see.

ADOLPHUS BASTABLE *enters. He is in evening dress, made in the latest fashion, with the right half of the coat and the left half of the trousers yellow and the other halves black. His silver-spangled waistcoat has a crimson handkerchief stuck between it and his shirt front.*

ADOLPHUS: What do you think of it?

LADY MAGNESIA: It is a dream! a creation! (*She turns him about to admire him.*)

ADOLPHUS (*proudly*): I shall never be mistaken for a waiter again.

FITZ: A drink, Adolphus?

ADOLPHUS: Thanks.

FITZTOLLEMACHE *goes to the cupboard and takes out a tray with tumblers and a bottle of whisky. He puts them on the dressing-table.*

FITZ: Is the gazogene full?

LADY MAGNESIA: Yes: you put in the powders yourself today.

FITZ (*sardonically*): So I did. The special powders! Ha! ha! ha! ha! ha! (*His face is again strangely variegated.*)

LADY MAGNESIA: Your complexion is really going to pieces. Why do you laugh in that silly way at nothing?

FITZ: Nothing! Ha, ha! Nothing! Ha, ha, ha!

ADOLPHUS: I hope, Mr Fitztollemache, you are not laughing at my clothes. I warn you that I am an Englishman. You may laugh at my manners, at my brains, at my national institutions; but if you laugh at my clothes, one of us must die.

Thunder.

FITZ: I laughed but at the irony of Fate. (*He takes a gazogene from the cupboard.*)

ADOLPHUS (*satisfied*): Oh, that! Oh, yes, of course!

FITZ: Let us drown all unkindness in a loving cup. (*He puts the gazogene on the floor in the middle of the room.*) Pardon the absence of a table: we found it in the way and pawned it. (*He takes the whisky bottle from the dressing-table.*)

LADY MAGNESIA: We picnic at home now. It is delightful.
She takes three tumblers from the dressing-table and sits on the floor, presiding over the gazogene, with Fitz and Adolphus squatting on her left and right respectively. FITZ *pours whisky into the tumblers.*

FITZ (*as* MAGNESIA *is about to squirt soda into his tumbler*): Stay! No soda for me. Let Adolphus have it all – all. I will take mine neat.

LADY MAGNESIA (*proffering tumbler to Adolphus*): Pledge me, Adolphus.

FITZ: Kiss the cup, Magnesia. Pledge her, man. Drink deep.

ADOLPHUS: To Magnesia!

FITZ: To Magnesia! (*The two men drink.*) It is done. (*Scrambling to his feet.*) Adolphus: you have but ten minutes to live – if so long.

ADOLPHUS: What mean you?

MAGNESIA (*rising*): My mind misgives me. I have a strange feeling here. (*Touching her heart.*)

ADOLPHUS: So have I, but lower down. (*Touching his stomach.*) That gazogene is disagreeing with me.

FITZ: It was poisoned!
Sensation.

ADOLPHUS (*rising*): Help! Police!

FITZ: Dastard! you would appeal to the law! Can you not die like a gentleman?

ADOLPHUS: But so young! when I have only worn my new clothes once.

MAGNESIA: It is too horrible. (*To Fitz.*) Fiend! what drove you to this wicked deed?

FITZ: Jealousy. You admired his clothes: you did not admire mine.

ADOLPHUS: My clothes! (*His face lights up with heavenly radiance.*) Have I indeed been found worthy to be the first clothes-martyr? Welcome, death! Hark! angels call me. (*The celestial choir again raises its favourite chant. He listens with a rapt expression.*

Suddenly the angels sing out of tune; and the radiance on the poisoned man's face turns a sickly green.) Yah – ah! Oh – ahoo! The gazogene is disagreeing extremely. Oh! (*He throws himself on the bed, writhing.*)

MAGNESIA (*to Fitz*): Monster: what have you done? (*She points to the distorted figure on the bed.*) That was once a Man, beautiful and glorious. What have you made of it? A writhing, agonized, miserable, moribund worm.

ADOLPHUS (*in a tone of the strongest remonstrance*): Oh, I say! Oh, come! No: look here, Magnesia! Really!

MAGNESIA: Oh, is this a time for petty vanity? Think of your misspent life —

ADOLPHUS (*much injured*): Whose misspent life?

MAGNESIA (*continuing relentlessly*): Look into your conscience: look into your stomach. (ADOLPHUS *collapses in hideous spasms. She turns to Fitz.*) And this is your handiwork!

FITZ: Mine is a passionate nature, Magnesia. I must have your undivided love. I must have your love: do you hear? LOVE! LOVE!! LOVE!!! LOVE!!!! LOVE!!!!!

He raves, accompanied by a fresh paroxysm from the victim on the bed.

MAGNESIA (*with sudden resolution*): You shall have it.

FITZ (*enraptured*): Magnesia! I have recovered your love! Oh, how slight appears the sacrifice of this man compared to so glorious a reward! I would poison ten men without a thought of self to gain one smile from you.

ADOLPHUS (*in a broken voice*): Farewell, Magnesia: my last hour is at hand. Farewell, farewell, farewell!

MAGNESIA: At this supreme moment, George Fitztollemache, I solemnly dedicate to you all that I formerly dedicated to poor Adolphus.

ADOLPHUS: Oh, please not poor Adolphus yet. I still live, you know.

MAGNESIA: The vital spark but flashes before it vanishes. (ADOLPHUS *groans.*) And now, Adolphus, take this last comfort from the unhappy Magnesia Fitztollemache. As I have dedicated to George all that I gave you, so I will bury in your grave – or in your urn if you are cremated – all that I gave to him.

FITZ: I hardly follow this.

MAGNESIA: I will explain. George: hitherto I have given Adolphus all the romance of my nature – all my love – all my dreams – all my caresses. Henceforth they are yours!

FITZ: Angel!

MAGNESIA: Adolphus: forgive me if this pains you.

ADOLPHUS: Don't mention it. I hardly feel it. The gazogene is so much worse. (*Taken bad again.*) Oh!

MAGNESIA: Peace, poor sufferer: there is still some balm. You are about to hear what I am going to dedicate to you.

ADOLPHUS: All I ask is a peppermint lozenge, for mercy's sake.

MAGNESIA: I have something far better than any lozenge: the devotion of a lifetime. Formerly it was George's. I kept his house, or rather, his lodgings. I mended his clothes. I darned his socks. I bought his food. I interviewed his creditors. I stood between him and the servants. I administered his domestic finances. When his hair needed cutting or his countenance was imperfectly washed, I pointed it out to him. The trouble that all this gave me made him prosaic in my eyes. Familiarity bred contempt. Now all that shall end. My husband shall be my hero, my lover, my perfect knight. He shall shield me from all care and trouble. He shall ask nothing in return but love – boundless, priceless, rapturous, soul-enthralling love, LOVE! LOVE!! LOVE!!! (*She raves and flings her arms about Fitz.*) And the duties I formerly discharged shall be replaced by the one supreme duty of duties: the duty of weeping at Adolphus's tomb.

FITZ (*reflectively*): My ownest, this sacrifice makes me feel that I have perhaps been a little selfish. I cannot help feeling that there is much to be said for the old arrangement. Why should Adolphus die for my sake?

ADOLPHUS: I am not dying for your sake, Fitz. I am dying because you poisoned me.

MAGNESIA: You do not fear to die, Adolphus, do you?

ADOLPHUS: N-n-no, I don't exactly fear to die. Still —

FITZ: Still, if an antidote —

ADOLPHUS (*bounding from the bed*): Antidote!

MAGNESIA (*with wild hope*): Antidote!

FITZ: If an antidote would not be too much of an anti-climax.

ADOLPHUS: Anti-climax be blowed! Do you think I am going to die to please the critics? Out with your antidote. Quick!

FITZ: The best antidote to the poison I have given you is lime, plenty of lime.

ADOLPHUS: Lime! You mock me! Do you think I carry lime about in my pockets?

FITZ: There is the plaster ceiling.

MAGNESIA: Yes, the ceiling. Saved, saved, saved!

All three frantically shy boots at the ceiling. Flakes of plaster rain down which ADOLPHUS *devours, at first ravenously, then with a marked falling off in relish.*

MAGNESIA (*picking up a huge slice*): Take this, Adolphus: it is the largest. (*She crams it into his mouth.*)

FITZ: Ha! a lump off the cornice! Try this.

ADOLPHUS (*desperately*): Stop! stop!

MAGNESIA: Do not stop. You will die. (*She tries to stuff him again.*)

ADOLPHUS (*resolutely*): I prefer death.

MAGNESIA and FITZ (*throwing themselves on their knees on either side of him*): For our sakes, Adolphus, persevere.

ADOLPHUS: No: unless you can supply lime in liquid form, I must perish. Finish that ceiling I cannot and will not.

MAGNESIA: I have a thought — an inspiration. My bust. (*She snatches it from its pedestal and brings it to him.*)

ADOLPHUS (*gazing fondly at it*): Can I resist it?

FITZ: Try the bun.

ADOLPHUS (*gnawing the knot of hair at the back of the bust's head: it makes him ill*): Yah, I cannot. I cannot. Not even your bust, Magnesia. Do not ask me. Let me die.

FITZ (*pressing the bust on him*): Force yourself to take a mouthful. Down with it, Adolphus!

ADOLPHUS: Useless. It would not stay down. Water! Some fluid! Ring for something to drink. (*He chokes.*)

MAGNESIA: I will save you. (*She rushes to the bell and rings.*)

PHYLLIS, *in her night-gown, with her hair prettily made up into a chevaux de frise of crocuses with pink and yellow curl papers, rushes in straight to Magnesia.*

PHYLLIS (*hysterically*): My beloved mistress, once more we meet. (*She sees Fitztollemache and screams.*) Ah! ah! ah! A Man! (*She sees Adolphus.*) Men!! (*She flies; but* FITZTOLLEMACHE *seizes her by the night-gown just as she is escaping.*) Unhand me, villain!

FITZ: This is no time for prudery, girl. Mr Bastable is dying.

PHYLLIS (*with concern*): Indeed, sir? I hope he will not think it unfeeling of me to appear at his deathbed in curl papers.

MAGNESIA: We know you have a good heart, Phyllis. Take this (*Giving her the bust*); dissolve it in a jug of hot water; and bring it back instantly. Mr Bastable's life depends on your haste.

PHYLLIS (*hesitating*): It do seem a pity, don't it, my lady, to spoil your lovely bust?

ADOLPHUS: Tush! This craze for fine art is beyond all bounds. Off with you. (*He pushes her out.*) Drink, drink, drink? My entrails are parched. Drink! (*He rushes deliriously to the gazogene.*)

FITZ (*rushing after him*): Madman, you forget! It is poisoned!

ADOLPHUS: I don't care. Drink, drink ! (*They wrestle madly for the gazogene. In the struggle they squirt all its contents away, mostly into one another's face.* ADOLPHUS *at last flings Fitztollemache to the floor, and puts the spout into his mouth.*) Empty! empty! (*With a shriek of despair he collapses on the bed, clasping the gazogene like a baby, and weeping over it.*)

FITZ (*aside to Magnesia*): Magnesia: I have always pretended not to notice it; but you keep a siphon for your private use in my hatbox.

MAGNESIA: I use it for washing old lace; but no matter: he shall have it. (*She produces a siphon from the hatbox, and offers a tumbler of soda-water to Adolphus.*)

ADOLPHUS: Thanks, thanks, oh, thanks! (*He drinks, A terrific fizzing is heard. He starts up screaming.*) Help! help! The ceiling is effervescing! I am BURSTING! (*He wallows convulsively on the bed.*)

FITZ: Quick! the rug strap! (*They pack him with blankets and strap him.*) Is that tight enough?

MAGNESIA (*anxiously*): Will you hold, do you think?

ADOLPHUS: The peril is past. The soda-water has gone flat.

MAGNESIA and FITZ: Thank heaven!

PHYLLIS *returns with a washstand ewer, in which she has dissolved the bust.*

MAGNESIA (*snatching it*): At last!

FITZ: You are saved. Drain it to the dregs.

FITZTOLLEMACHE *holds the lip of the ewer to Adolphus's mouth and gradually raises it until it stands upside down.* ADOLPHUS'S *efforts to swallow it are fearful,* PHYLLIS *thumping his back when he chokes, and* MAGNESIA *loosening the straps when he moans. At last, with a sigh of relief, he sinks back in the women's arms.* FITZ *shakes the empty ewer upside down like a potman shaking the froth out of a flagon.*

ADOLPHUS: How inexpressibly soothing to the chest! A delicious numbness steals through all my members. I would sleep.

MAGNESIA
FITZ } (*whispering*: Let him sleep.
PHYLLIS

He sleeps. Celestial harps are heard; but their chords cease on the abrupt entrance of the landlord, a vulgar person in pyjamas.

THE LANDLORD: Eah! Eah! Wot's this? Wot's all this noise? Ah kin ennybody sleep through it? (*Looking at the floor and ceiling.*) Ellow! wot you bin doin te maw ceilin?

FITZ: Silence, or leave the room. If you wake that man he dies.

THE LANDLORD: If 'e kin sleep through the noise you three mikes 'e kin sleep through ennythink.

MAGNESIA: Detestable vulgarian: your pronunciation jars on the finest chords of my nature. Begone!

THE LANDLORD (*looking at Adolphus*): Aw downt blieve eze

esleep. Aw blieve eze dead. (*Calling.*) Pleece! Pleece! Merder!
(*A blue halo plays mysteriously on the door, which opens and reveals a
policeman. Thunder.*) Eah, pleecmin: these three's bin an merdered
this gent between em, an naw tore moy ahse dahn.

THE POLICEMAN (*offended*): Policeman, indeed! Where's your
manners?

FITZ: Officer —

THE POLICEMAN (*with distinguished consideration*): Sir?

FITZ: As between gentlemen —

THE POLICEMAN (*bowing*): Sir: to you.

FITZ (*bowing*): I may inform you that my friend had an acute
attack of indigestion. No carbonate of soda being available,
he swallowed a portion of this man's ceiling. (*Pointing to
Adolphus.*) Behold the result!

THE POLICEMAN: The ceiling was poisoned! Well, of all the
artful — (*He collars the landlord.*) I arrest you for wilful murder.

THE LANDLORD (*appealing to the heavens*): Ow, is this jestice!
Ah could aw tell 'e wiz gowin' te eat moy ceilin'?

THE POLICEMAN (*releasing him*): True. The case is more com-
plicated than I thought. (*He tries to lift Adolphus's arm but
cannot.*) Stiff already.

THE LANDLORD (*trying to lift Adolphus's leg*): An' precious
'evvy. (*Feeling the calf.*) Woy, eze gorn 'ez awd ez niles.

FITZ (*rushing to the bed*): What is this?

MAGNESIA: Oh, say not he is dead. Phyllis: fetch a doctor.
(*PHYLLIS runs out. They all try to lift Adolphus; but he is perfectly
stiff, and as heavy as lead.*) Rouse him. Shake him.

THE POLICEMAN (*exhausted*): Whew! Is he a man or a statue?
(*MAGNESIA utters a piercing scream.*) What's wrong, Miss?

MAGNESIA (*to Fitz*): Do you not see what has happened?

FITZ (*striking his forehead*): Horror on horror's head!

THE LANDLORD: Wotjemean?

MAGNESIA: The plaster has set inside him. The officer was right:
he is indeed a living statue.

MAGNESIA *flings herself on the stony breast of Adolphus.* FITZ-
TOLLEMACHE *buries his head in his hands; and his chest heaves*

C

convulsively. The policeman takes a small volume from his pocket and consults it.

THE POLICEMAN: This case is not provided for in my book of instructions. It don't seem no use trying artificial respiration, do it? (*To the landlord.*) Here! lend a hand, you. We'd best take him and set him up in Trafalgar Square.

THE LANDLORD: Aushd pat 'im in the cestern an worsh it aht of 'im.

PHYLLIS *comes back with a Doctor.*

PHYLLIS: The medical man, my lady.

THE POLICEMAN: A poison case, sir.

THE DOCTOR: Do you mean to say that an unqualified person! a layman! has dared to administer poison in my district?

THE POLICEMAN (*raising Magnesia tenderly*): It looks like it. Hold up, my lady.

THE DOCTOR: Not a moment must be lost. The patient must be kept awake at all costs. Constant and violent motion is necessary.

He snatches Magnesia from the Policeman, and rushes her about the room.

FITZ: Stop! That is not the poisoned person!

THE DOCTOR: It is you, then. Why did you not say so before?

He seizes Fitztollemache and rushes him about.

THE LANDLORD: Naow, naow, thet ynt 'im.

THE DOCTOR: What, you!

He pounces on the Landlord and rushes him round.

THE LANDLORD: Eah! chack it. (*He trips the Doctor up. Both fall.*) Jes owld this leeonatic, will you, Mister Horficer?

THE POLICEMAN (*dragging both of them to their feet*): Come out of it, will you. You must all come with me to the station.

Thunder.

MAGNESIA: What! In this frightful storm!

The hail patters noisily on the window.

PHYLLIS: I think it's raining.

The wind howls.

THE LANDLORD: It's thanderin' and lawtnin'.

FITZ: It's dangerous.

THE POLICEMAN (*drawing his baton and whistle*): If you won't come quietly, then —

He whistles. A fearful flash is followed by an appalling explosion of heaven's artillery. A thunderbolt enters the room, and strikes the helmet of the devoted constable, whence it is attracted to the waistcoat of the doctor by the lancet in his pocket. Finally it leaps with fearful force on the landlord, who, being of a gross and spongy nature, absorbs the electric fluid at the cost of his life. The others look on horror-stricken as the three victims, after reeling, jostling, cannoning through a ghastly quadrille, at last sink inanimate on the carpet.

MAGNESIA (*listening at the doctor's chest*): Dead!

FITZ (*kneeling by the landlord, and raising his hand, which drops with a thud*): Dead!

PHYLLIS (*seizing the looking-glass and holding it to the Policeman's lips*): Dead!

FITZ (*solemnly rising*): The copper attracted the lightning.

MAGNESIA (*rising*): After life's fitful fever they sleep well. Phyllis: sweep them up.

PHYLLIS replaces the looking-glass on the dressing-table; takes up the fan; and fans the POLICEMAN, who rolls away like a leaf before the wind to the wall. She disposes similarly of the landlord and doctor.

PHYLLIS: Will they be in your way if I leave them there until morning, my lady? Or shall I bring up the ashpan and take them away?

MAGNESIA: They will not disturb us. Goodnight, Phyllis.

PHYLLIS: Goodnight, my lady. Goodnight, sir.

She retires.

MAGNESIA: And now, husband, let us perform our last sad duty to our friend. He has become his own monument. Let us erect him. He is heavy; but love can do much.

FITZ: A little leverage will get him on his feet. Give me my umbrella.

MAGNESIA: True.

She hands him the umbrella, and takes up the bootjack. They get them under Adolphus's back, and prise him up on his feet.

FITZ: That's done it! Whew!

MAGNESIA (*kneeling at the left hand of the statue*): For ever and for ever, Adolphus.

FITZ (*kneeling at the right hand of the statue*): The rest is silence.

The Angels sing Bill Bailey. *The statue raises its hands in an attitude of blessing, and turns its limelit face to heaven as the curtain falls. National Anthem.*

The Shewing-up of Blanco Posnet

A Sermon in Crude Melodrama

The toleration of heresy and shocks to morality on the stage, and even their protection against the prejudices and superstitions which necessarily enter into morality and public opinion, are essential to the welfare of the nation.

CHARACTERS

BLANCO POSNET, *charged with horse-stealing*
ELDER DANIELS, *his step-brother*
SHERIFF KEMP
STRAPPER KEMP, *the Sheriff's younger brother*
WAGGONER JO, *a carter*
FOREMAN OF THE JURY
NESTOR, *a Juryman*
TEN OTHER JURYMEN
FEEMY EVANS
THE MOTHER
BABSY
LOTTIE
HANNAH
JESSIE
EMMA
OTHER MEN AND WOMEN IN CROWD

SCENE: The United States of America – the Wild West: a Barn in use as a Courthouse.

TIME: The beginning of the century.

THE SHEWING-UP OF BLANCO POSNET

It comes as a surprise to many people to learn that so dynamic and colourful a character as Shaw fell foul of the censor on only three occasions. He put such controversial ideas over through the mouthpieces of his characters that he must often have been a thorn in the flesh of authority. The three plays that were banned were *Mrs Warren's Profession*, because of its theme, although this was treated with good taste, sincerity and seriousness; *Press Cuttings*, because its political references and thinly disguised caricatures of Asquith (then Prime Minister) and General Kitchener, gave offence; and *The Shewing-up of Blanco Posnet*, because its references to the Deity were regarded as blasphemous (no objections were raised against the morals of the characters – much more open to question!).

Shaw seized the opportunity in a printed version of *The Shewing-up of Blanco Posnet* to write at length against the office of the censor. At least the banning of these plays obliged Parliament to set up an inquiry into the workings of the censorship; so to that extent it was a good thing. All three banned plays were performed privately by the Stage Society; and, in the case of *Press Cuttings*, a public performance was soon allowed when the names of the two chief characters were changed to Bones and Johnson! Authority was thus placated! Public performances were, of course, possible in the United States. *The Shewing-up of Blanco Posnet*, however, had its first public performance in Dublin in 1909; not until 1916 was it licensed for public performance in this country. *Mrs Warren's Profession* had to wait till 1925 for a stage licence to be seen by English audiences, though translations had been seen in most European countries by then.

The Shewing-up of Blanco Posnet shows Shaw's versatility. It was his only play on a Wild West theme. But it was not his only play with an American setting, for *The Devil's Disciple* was set in the period of the American War of Independence. These two plays have another thing in common: both deal with the redemption of a 'bad man', redemption brought about by an act of human kindness that is in the nature of a spiritual conversion. Many critics claim that the shorter play is the greater of the two, and that, just as Shaw wrote *The Man of Destiny* to prepare himself for the longer *Caesar and Cleopatra*, so he wrote *The Shewing-up of Blanco Posnet* after exploring a similar theme at greater length in *The Devil's Disciple*. The religious and moral overtones of the play were not far from Shaw's mind when he subtitled it *A Sermon in Crude Melodrama*. In a preface he called it a 'religious tract in dramatic form'. And for several years this same play was banned as blasphemous!

THE SHEWING-UP OF BLANCO POSNET

A number of women are sitting together in a big room not unlike an old English tithe barn in its timbered construction, but with windows high up next to the roof. It is furnished as a courthouse, with the floor raised next the walls, and on this raised flooring a seat for the Sheriff, a rough jury box on his right, and a bar to put prisoners to on his left. In the well in the middle is a table with benches round it. A few other benches are in disorder round the room. The autumn sun is shining warmly through the windows and the open door. The women, whose dress and speech are those of pioneers of civilization in a territory of the United States of America, are seated round the table and on the benches, shucking nuts. The conversation is at its height.

BABSY (*a bumptious young slattern, with some good looks*): I say that a man that would steal a horse would do anything.

LOTTIE (*a sentimental girl, neat and clean*): Well, I never should look at it in that way. I do think killing a man is worse any day than stealing a horse.

HANNAH (*elderly and wise*): I don't say it's right to kill a man. In a place like this, where every man has to have a revolver, and where there's so much to try people's tempers, the men get to be a deal too free with one another in the way of shooting. God knows it's hard enough to have to bring a boy into the world and nurse him up to be a man only to have him brought home to you on a shutter, perhaps for nothing, or only just to show that the man that killed him wasn't afraid of him. But men are like children when they get a gun in their hands: they're not content 'til they've used it on somebody.

JESSIE (*a good-natured but sharp-tongued, hoity-toity young woman; BABSY'S rival in good looks and her superior in tidiness*): They

shoot for the love of it. Look at them at a lynching. They're
not content to hang the man; but directly the poor creature is
swung up they all shoot him full of holes, wasting their
cartridges that cost solid money, and pretending they do it in
horror of his wickedness, though half of them would have a
rope round their own necks if all they did was known. Let
alone the mess it makes.

LOTTIE: I wish we could get more civilized. I don't like all this
lynching and shooting. I don't believe any of us like it, if the
truth were known.

BABSY: Our Sheriff is a real strong man. You want a strong
man for a rough lot like our people here. He ain't afraid to
shoot and he ain't afraid to hang. Lucky for us quiet ones,
too.

JESSIE: Oh, don't talk to me. I know what men are. Of course
he ain't afraid to shoot and he ain't afraid to hang. Where's
the risk in that with the law on his side and the whole crowd
at his back longing for the lynching as if it was a spree? Would
one of them own to it or let him own to it if they lynched the
wrong man? Not them. What they call justice in this place is
nothing but a breaking out of the devil that's in all of us.
What I want to see is a Sheriff that ain't afraid not to shoot and
not to hang.

EMMA (*a sneak who sides with Babsy or Jessie, according to the fortune
of war*): Well, I must say it does sicken me to see Sheriff Kemp
putting down his foot, as he calls it. Why don't he put it
down on his wife? She wants it worse than half the men he
lynches. He and his Vigilance Committee, indeed!

BABSY (*incensed*): Oh, well! if people are going to take the part
of horse-thieves against the Sheriff —?

JESSIE: Who's taking the part of horse-thieves against the
Sheriff?

BABSY: You are. Waitle your own horse is stolen, and you'll
know better. I had an uncle that died of thirst in the sage brush
because a Negro stole his horse. But they caught him and
burned him; and serve him right, too.

EMMA: I have known a child that was born crooked because its mother had to do a horse's work that was stolen.

BABSY: There! You hear that? I say stealing a horse is ten times worse than killing a man. And if the Vigilance Committee ever gets hold of you, you'd better have killed twenty men than as much as stole a saddle or bridle, much less a horse.

ELDER DANIELS *comes in.*

ELDER DANIELS: Sorry to disturb you, ladies; but the Vigilance Committee has taken a prisoner, and they want the room to try him in.

JESSIE: But they can't try him 'til Sheriff Kemp comes back from the wharf.

ELDER DANIELS: Yes; but we have to keep the prisoner here 'til he comes.

BABSY: What do you want to put him here for? Can't you tie him up in the Sheriff's stable?

ELDER DANIELS: He has a soul to be saved, almost like the rest of us. I am bound to try to put some religion into him before he goes into his Maker's presence after the trial.

HANNAH: What has he done, Mr Daniels?

ELDER DANIELS: Stole a horse.

BABSY: And are we to be turned out of the town hall for a horse-thief? Ain't a stable good enough for his religion?

ELDER DANIELS: It may be good enough for his, Babsy; but, by your leave, it is not good enough for mine. While I am Elder here, I shall 'umbly endeavour to keep up the dignity of Him I serve to the best of my small ability. So I must ask you to be good enough to clear out. Allow me. (*He takes the sack of husks and puts it out of the way against the panels of the jury box.*)

THE WOMEN (*murmuring*): That's always the way. Just as we'd settled down to work. What harm are we doing? Well, it is tiresome. Let them finish the job themselves. Oh dear, oh dear! We can't have a minute to ourselves. Shoving us out like that!

HANNAH: Whose horse was it, Mr Daniels?

ELDER DANIELS (*returning to move the other sack*): I am sorry to

say it was the Sheriff's horse – the one he loaned to young
Strapper. Strapper loaned it to me; and the thief stole it,
thinking it was mine. If it had been mine, I'd have forgiven
him cheerfully. I'm sure I hoped he would get away; for he had
two hours start of the Vigilance Committee. But they caught
him. (*He disposes of the other sack also.*)

JESSIE: It can't have been much of a horse if they caught him
with two hours start.

ELDER DANIELS (*coming back to the centre of the group*): The
strange thing is that he wasn't on the horse when they took
him. He was walking; and of course he denies that he ever had
the horse. The Sheriff's brother wanted to tie him up and lash
him 'til he confessed what he'd done with it; but I couldn't
allow that: it's not the law.

BABSY: Law! What right has a horse-thief to any law? Law is
thrown away on a brute like that.

ELDER DANIELS: Don't say that, Babsy. No man should be
made to confess by cruelty until religion has been tried and
failed. Please God I'll get the whereabouts of the horse from
him if you'll be so good as to clear out from this. (*Disturbance.*)
They are bringing him in. Now, ladies! please, please.

They rise reluctantly. HANNAH, JESSIE, *and* LOTTIE *retreat to
the Sheriff's bench, shepherded by* DANIELS; *but the other women
crowd forward behind Babsy and Emma to see the prisoner.*

BLANCO POSNET *is brought in by* STRAPPER KEMP, *the Sheriff's
brother, and a cross-eyed man called* SQUINTY. *Others follow. Blanco
is evidently a blackguard. It would be necessary to clean him to make
a close guess at his age; but he is under forty, and an upturned, red
moustache, and the arrangement of his hair in a crest on his brow,
proclaim the dandy in spite of his intense disreputableness. He carries
his head high, and has a fairly resolute mouth, though the fire of
incipient delirium tremens is in his eye. His arms are bound with a
rope with a long end, which* SQUINTY *holds. They release him when
he enters; and he stretches himself and lounges across the courthouse in
front of the women.* STRAPPER *and the men remain between him and
the door.*

BABSY (*spitting at him as he passes her*): Horse-thief! horse-thief!

OTHERS: You will hang for it; do you hear? And serve you right. Serve you right. That will teach you. I wouldn't wait to try you. Lynch him straight off, the varmint. Yes, yes. Tell the boys. Lynch him.

BLANCO (*mocking*): 'Angels ever bright and fair —'

BABSY: You call me an angel, and I'll smack your dirty face for you.

BLANCO: 'Take, oh, take me to your care.'

EMMA: There won't be any angels where you're going to.

OTHERS: Aha! Devils, more likely. And too good company for a horse-thief.

ALL: Horse-thief! Horse-thief! Horse-thief!

BLANCO: Do women make the law here, or men? Drive these heifers out.

THE WOMEN: Oh! (*They rush at him, vituperating, screaming passionately, tearing at him.* LOTTIE *puts her fingers in her ears and runs out.* HANNAH *follows, shaking her head.* BLANCO *is thrown down.*) Oh, did you hear what he called us? You foul-mouthed brute! You liar! How dare you put such a name to a decent woman? Let me get at him. You coward! Oh, he struck me: did you see that? Lynch him! Pete, will you stand by and hear me called names by a skunk like that? Burn him: burn him! That's what I'd do with him. Aye, burn him!

THE MEN (*pulling the women away from* BLANCO, *and getting them out partly by violence and partly by coaxing*): Here! come out of this. Let him alone. Clear the courthouse. Come on now. Out with you. Now, Sally: out you go. Let go my hair, or I'll twist your arm out. Ah, would you? Now then: get along. You know you must go. What's the use of scratching like that? Now, ladies, ladies, ladies. How would you like it if you were going to be hanged?

At last the women are pushed out, leaving ELDER DANIELS, *the Sheriff's brother* STRAPPER KEMP, *and a few others with* BLANCO. STRAPPER *is a lad just turning into a man: strong, selfish, sulky, and determined.*

BLANCO (*sitting up and tidying himself*) —

> Oh woman, in our hours of ease,
> Uncertain, coy, and hard to please —

Is my face scratched? I can feel their damned claws all over me still. Am I bleeding? (*He sits on the nearest bench.*)

ELDER DANIELS: Nothing to hurt. They've drawn a drop or two under your left eye.

STRAPPER: Lucky for you to have an eye left in your head.

BLANCO (*wiping the blood off*) —

> When pain and anguish wring the brow,
> A ministering angel thou.

Go out to them, Strapper Kemp; and tell them about your big brother's little horse that some wicked man stole. Go and cry in your mammy's lap.

STRAPPER (*furious*): You jounce me any more about that horse, Blanco Posnet; and I'll – I'll —

BLANCO: You'll scratch my face, won't you? Yah! Your brother's the Sheriff, ain't he?

STRAPPER: Yes, he is. He hangs horse-thieves.

BLANCO (*with calm conviction*): He's a rotten Sheriff. Oh, a rotten Sheriff. If he did his first duty he'd hang himself. This is a rotten town. Your fathers came here on a false alarm of gold-digging; and when the gold didn't pan out, they lived by licking their young into habits of honest industry.

STRAPPER: If I hadn't promised Elder Daniels here to give him a chance to keep you out of Hell, I'd take the job of twisting your neck off the hands of the Vigilance Committee.

BLANCO (*with infinite scorn*): You and your rotten Elder, and your rotten Vigilance Committee!

STRAPPER: They're sound enough to hang a horse-thief, any-how.

BLANCO: Any fool can hang the wisest man in the country. Nothing he likes better. But you can't hang me.

STRAPPER: Can't we?

BLANCO: No, you can't. I left the town this morning before sunrise, because it's a rotten town, and I couldn't bear to see it in
the light. Your brother's horse did the same, as any sensible
horse would. Instead of going to look for the horse, you went
looking for me. That was a rotten thing to do, because the horse
belonged to your brother – or to the man he stole it from – and
I don't belong to him. Well, you found me; but you didn't find
the horse. If I had took the horse, I'd have been on the horse.
Would I have taken all that time to get to where I did if I'd a
horse to carry me?

STRAPPER: I don't believe you started not for two hours after
you say you did.

BLANCO: Who cares what you believe or don't believe? Is a man
worth six of you to be hanged because you've lost your big
brother's horse, and you'll want to kill somebody to relieve
your rotten feelings when he licks you for it? Not likely. 'Til
you can find a witness that saw me with that horse you can't
touch me; and you know it.

STRAPPER: Is that the law, Elder?

ELDER DANIELS: The Sheriff knows the law. I wouldn't say for
sure; but I think it would be more seemly to have a witness. Go
and round one up, Strapper; and leave me here alone to wrestle
with his poor blinded soul.

STRAPPER: I'll get a witness all right enough. I know the road he
took; and I'll ask at every house within sight of it for a mile out.
Come, boys.

STRAPPER *goes out with the others, leaving* BLANCO *and* ELDER
DANIELS *together.* BLANCO *rises and strolls over to the Elder,*
surveying him with extreme disparagement.

BLANCO: Well, brother? Well, Boozy Posnet, alias Elder
Daniels? Well, thief? Well, drunkard?

ELDER DANIELS: It's no good, Blanco. They'll never believe
we're brothers.

BLANCO: Never fear. Do you suppose I want to claim you? Do
you suppose I'm proud of you? You're a rotten brother,
Boozy Posnet. All you ever did when I owned you was to

borrow money from me to get drunk with. Now you lend money and sell drink to other people. I was ashamed of you before; and I'm worse ashamed of you now. I won't have you for a brother. Heaven gave you to me; but I return the blessing without thanks. So be easy: I shan't blab. (*He turns his back on him and sits down.*)

ELDER DANIELS: I tell you they wouldn't believe you; so what does it matter to me whether you blab or not? Talk sense, Blanco: there's no time for your foolery now; for you'll be a dead man an hour after the Sheriff comes back. What possessed you to steal that horse?

BLANCO: I didn't steal it. I distrained on it for what you owed me. I thought it was yours. I was a fool to think that you owned anything but other people's property. You laid your hands on everything father and mother had when they died. I never asked you for a fair share. I never asked you for all the money I'd lent you from time to time. I asked you for mother's old necklace with the hair locket in it. You wouldn't give me that: you wouldn't give me anything. So as you refused me my due I took it, just to give you a lesson.

ELDER DANIELS: Why didn't you take the necklace if you must steal something? They wouldn't have hanged you for that.

BLANCO: Perhaps I'd rather be hanged for stealing a horse than let off for a damned piece of sentimentality.

ELDER DANIELS: Oh, Blanco, Blanco: spiritual pride has been your ruin. If you'd only done like me, you'd be a free and respectable man this day instead of laying there with a rope round your neck.

BLANCO (*turning on him*): Done like you! What do you mean? Drink like you, eh? Well I've done some of that lately. I see things.

ELDER DANIELS: Too late, Blanco: too late. (*Convulsively.*) Oh, why didn't you drink as I used to? Why didn't you drink as I was led by the Lord for my good, until the time came for me to give it up? It was drink that saved my character when I was a

young man; and it was the want of it that spoiled yours. Tell me
this. Did I ever get drunk when I was working?

BLANCO: No; but then you never worked when you had money
enough to get drunk.

ELDER DANIELS: That just shows the wisdom of Providence
and the Lord's mercy. God fulfils Himself in many ways: ways
we little think of when we try to set up our own shortsighted
laws against His Word. When does the Devil catch hold of a
man? Not when he's working and not when he's drunk; but
when he's idle and sober. Our own natures tell us to drink
when we have nothing else to do. Look at you and me! When
we'd both earned a pocketful of money, what did we do? Went
on the spree, naturally. But I was humble minded. I did as the
rest did. I gave my money in at the drink-shop; and I said, 'Fire
me out when I have drunk it all up.' Did you ever see me sober
while it lasted?

BLANCO: No; and you looked so disgusting that I wonder it
didn't set me against drink for the rest of my life.

ELDER DANIELS: That was your spiritual pride, Blanco. You
never reflected that when I was drunk I was in a state of
innocence. Temptations and bad company and evil thoughts
passed by me like the summer wind as you might say: I was too
drunk to notice them. When the money was gone, and they
fired me out, I was fired out like gold out of the furnace, with
my character unspoiled and unspotted; and when I went back
to work, the work kept me steady. Can you say as much,
Blanco? Did your holidays leave your character unspoiled? Oh,
no, no. It was theatres: it was gambling: it was evil company:
it was reading vain romances: it was women, Blanco, women:
it was wrong thoughts and gnawing discontent. It ended in
your becoming a rambler and a gambler: it is going to end this
evening on the gallows tree. Oh, what a lesson against spiritual
pride! Oh, what a — (BLANCO *throws his hat at him.*)

BLANCO: Stow it, Boozy. Sling it. Cut it. Cheese it. Shut up.
'Shake not the dying sinner's sand.'

ELDER DANIELS: Aye: there you go, with your scraps of lustful poetry. But you can't deny what I tell you. Why, do you think I would put my soul in peril by selling drink if I thought it did no good, as them silly temperance reformers make out, flying in the face of the natural tastes implanted in us all for a good purpose? Not if I was to starve for it tomorrow. But I know better. I tell you, Blanco, what keeps America today the purest of the nations is that when she's not working she's too drunk to hear the voice of the tempter.

BLANCO: Don't deceive yourself, Boozy. You sell drink because you make a bigger profit out of it than you can by selling tea. And you gave up drink yourself because when you got that fit at Edwardstown the doctor told you you'd die the next time; and that frightened you off it.

ELDER DANIELS (*fervently*): Oh thank God selling drink pays me! And thank God He sent me that fit as a warning that my drinking time was past and gone, and that He needed me for another service!

BLANCO: Take care, Boozy. He hasn't finished with you yet. He always has a trick up His sleeve —

ELDER DANIELS: Oh, is that the way to speak of the ruler of the universe – the great and almighty God?

BLANCO: He's a sly one. He's a mean one. He lies low for you. He plays cat and mouse with you. He lets you run loose until you think you're shut of Him; and then, when you least expect it, He's got you.

ELDER DANIELS: Speak more respectful, Blanco – more reverent.

BLANCO (*springing up and coming at him*): Reverent! Who taught you your reverent cant? Not your Bible. It says He cometh like a thief in the night – aye, like a thief – a horse-thief —

ELDER DANIELS (*shocked*): Oh!

BLANCO (*overbearing him*): And it's true. That's how He caught me and put my neck into the halter. To spite me because I had no use for Him – because I lived my own life in my own way, and would have no truck with His 'Don't do this,' and 'You mustn't do that,' and 'You'll go to Hell if you do the other.' I

gave Him the go-by and did without Him all these years. But
He caught me out at last. The laugh is with Him as far as
hanging me goes. (*He thrusts his hands into his pockets and lunges
moodily away from* DANIELS, *to the table, where he sits facing the
jury box*).

ELDER DANIELS: Don't dare to put your theft on Him, man.
It was the Devil tempted you to steal the horse.

BLANCO: Not a bit of it. Neither God nor Devil tempted me to
take the horse: I took it on my own. He had a cleverer trick
than that ready for me. (*He takes his hands out of his pockets and
clenches his fists.*) Gosh! When I think that I might have been safe
and fifty miles away by now with that horse; and here I am
waiting to be hung up and filled with lead! What came to me?
What made me such a fool? That's what I want to know. That's
the great secret.

ELDER DANIELS (*at the opposite side of the table*): Blanco: the great
secret now is, what did you do with the horse?

BLANCO (*striking the table with his fist*): May my lips be blighted
like my soul if ever I tell that to you or any mortal man! They
may roast me alive or cut me to ribbons; but Strapper Kemp
shall never have the laugh on me over that job. Let them hang
me. Let them shoot. So long as they are shooting a man and not
a snivelling skunk and softy, I can stand up to them and take all
they can give me – game.

ELDER DANIELS: Don't be headstrong, Blanco. What's the use?
(*Slyly.*) They might let up on you if you put Strapper in the way
of getting his brother's horse back.

BLANCO: Not they. Hanging's too big a treat for them to give up
a fair chance. I've done it myself. I've yelled with the dirtiest of
them when a man no worse than myself was swung up. I've
emptied my revolver into him, and persuaded myself that he
deserved it and that I was doing justice with strong stern men.
Well, my turn's come now. Let the men I yelled at and shot at
look up out of Hell and see the boys yelling and shooting at me
as *I* swing up.

ELDER DANIELS: Well, even if you want to be hanged, is that

any reason why Strapper shouldn't have his horse? I tell you I'm responsible to him for it. (*Bending over the table coaxing him.*) Act like a brother, Blanco: tell me what you done with it.

BLANCO (*shortly, getting up, and leaving the table*): Never you mind what I done with it. I was done out of it: let that be enough for you.

ELDER DANIELS (*following him*): Then why don't you put us on to the man that done you out of it?

BLANCO: Because he'd be too clever for you, just as he was too clever for me.

ELDER DANIELS: Make your mind easy about that, Blanco. He won't be too clever for the boys and Sheriff Kemp if you put them on his trail.

BLANCO: Yes, he will. It wasn't a man.

ELDER DANIELS: Then what was it?

BLANCO (*pointing upward*): Him.

ELDER DANIELS: Oh what a way to utter His holy name!

BLANCO: He done me out of it. He meant to pay off old scores by bringing me here. He means to win the deal and you can't stop Him. Well, He's made a fool of me; but He can't frighten me. I'm not going to beg off. I'll fight off if I get a chance. I'll lie off if they can't get a witness against me. But back down I never will, not if all the hosts of heaven come to snivel at me in white surplices and offer me my life in exchange for an 'umble and a contrite heart.

ELDER DANIELS: You're not in your right mind, Blanco. I'll tell 'em you're mad. I believe they'll let you off on that. (*He makes for the door.*)

BLANCO (*seizing him, with horror in his eyes*): Don't go: don't leave me alone: do you hear?

ELDER DANIELS: Has your conscience brought you to this that you're afraid to be left alone in broad daylight, like a child in the dark.

BLANCO: I'm afraid of Him and His tricks. When I have you to raise the devil in me – when I have people to show off before and keep me game, I'm all right; but I've lost my nerve for being alone since this morning. It's when you're alone that He take His advantage. He might turn my head again. He might send people to me – not real people perhaps. (*Shivering.*) By God, I don't believe that woman and the child were real. I don't. I never noticed them 'til they were at my elbow.

ELDER DANIELS: What woman and what child? What are you talking about? Have you been drinking too hard?

BLANCO: Never you mind. You've got to stay with me: that's all; or else send someone else – someone rottener than yourself to keep the devil in me. Strapper Kemp will do. Or a few of those scratching devils of women.

STRAPPER KEMP *comes back.*

ELDER DANIELS (*to* STRAPPER): He's gone off his head.

STRAPPER: Foxing, more likely. (*Going past* DANIELS *and talking to* BLANCO *nose to nose.*) It's no good: we hang madmen here; and a good job too!

BLANCO: I feel safe with you, Strapper. You're one of the rottenest.

STRAPPER: You know you're done, and that you may as well be hanged for a sheep as a lamb. So talk away. I've got my witness; and I'll trouble you not to make a move towards her when she comes in to identify you.

BLANCO (*retreating in terror*): A woman? She ain't real: neither is the child.

ELDER DANIELS: He's raving about a woman and a child. I tell he's gone off his chump.

STRAPPER (*calling to those without*): Show the lady in there.

FEEMY EVANS *comes in. She is a young woman of twenty-three or twenty-four, with impudent manners, battered good looks, and dirty-fine dress.*

ELDER DANIELS: Morning, Feemy.

FEEMY: Morning, Elder. (*She passes on and slips her arm familiarly through* STRAPPER'S.)

STRAPPER: Ever see him before, Feemy?

FEEMY: That's the little lot that was on your horse this morning, Strapper. Not a doubt of it.

BLANCO (*implacably contemptuous*): Go home and wash yourself, you slut.

FEEMY (*reddening and disengaging her arm from* STRAPPER'S): I'm clean enough to hang you, anyway. (*Going over to him threateningly.*) You're no true American man, to insult a woman like that.

BLANCO: A woman! Oh Lord! You saw me on a horse, did you?

FEEMY: Yes, I did.

BLANCO: Got up early on purpose to do it, didn't you?

FEEMY: No I didn't: I stayed up late on a spree.

BLANCO: I was on a horse, was I?

FEEMY: Yes you were; and if you deny it you're a liar.

BLANCO (*to* STRAPPER): She saw a man on a horse when she was too drunk to tell which was the man and which was the horse —

FEEMY (*breaking in*): You lie. I wasn't drunk – at least not as drunk as that.

BLANCO (*ignoring the interruption*) – and you found a man without a horse. Is a man on a horse the same as a man on foot? Yah! Take your witness away. Who's going to believe her? Throw her out on the dump. You've got to find that horse before you get a rope round my neck. (*He turns away from her contemptuously, and sits at the table with his back to the jury box.*)

FEEMY (*following him*): I'll hang you, you dirty horse-thief; or not a man in this camp will ever get a word or a look from me again. You're just trash: that's what you are. White trash.

BLANCO: And what are you, darling? What are you? You're a worse danger to a town like this than ten horse-thieves.

FEEMY: Mr Kemp: will you stand by and hear me insulted in that low way? (*To* BLANCO, *spitefully.*) I'll see you swung up and I'll see you cut down: I'll see you high and I'll see you low, as dangerous as I am. (*He laughs.*) Oh you needn't try to brazen it out. You'll look white enough before the boys are done with you.

BLANCO: You do me good, Feemy. Stay by me to the end, won't you? Hold my hand to the last; and I'll die game. (*He puts out his hand: she strikes savagely at it; but he withdraws it in time and laughs at her discomfiture.*)

FEEMY: You —

ELDER DANIELS: Never mind him, Feemy: he's not right in his head today. (*She receives the assurance with contemptuous incredulity, and sits down on the step of the Sheriff's dais.*)

SHERIFF KEMP *comes in: a stout man, with large flat ears, and a neck thicker than his head.*

ELDER DANIELS: Morning, Sheriff.

THE SHERIFF: Morning, Elder. (*Passing on.*) Morning, Strapper. (*Passing on.*) Morning, Miss Evans. (*Stopping between Strapper and* BLANCO.) Is this the prisoner?

BLANCO (*rising*): That's so. Morning, Sheriff.

THE SHERIFF: Morning. You know, I suppose, that if you've stole a horse and the jury find against you, you won't have any time to settle your affairs. Consequently, if you feel guilty, you'd better settle 'em now.

BLANCO: Affairs be damned! I've got none.

THE SHERIFF: Well, are you in a proper state of mind? Has the Elder talked to you?

BLANCO: He has. And I say it's against the law. It's torture; that's what it is.

ELDER DANIELS: He's not accountable. He's out of his mind, Sheriff. He's not fit to go into the presence of his Maker.

THE SHERIFF: You are a merciful man, Elder; but you won't take the boys with you there. (*To* BLANCO.) If it comes to hanging you, you'd better for your own sake be hanged in a proper state of mind than in an improper one. But it won't make any difference to us: make no mistake about that.

BLANCO: Lord keep me wicked 'til I die! Now I've said my little prayer. I'm ready. Not that I'm guilty, mind you; but this is a rotten town, dead certain to do the wrong thing.

THE SHERIFF: You won't be asked to live long in it, I guess. (*To* STRAPPER.) Got the witness all right, Strapper?

STRAPPER: Yes, got everything.

BLANCO: Except the horse.

THE SHERIFF: What's that? Ain't you got the horse?

STRAPPER: No. He traded it before we overtook him, I guess. But Feemy saw him on it.

FEEMY: She did.

STRAPPER: Shall I call in the boys?

BLANCO: Just a moment, Sheriff. A good appearance is everything in a low-class place like this. (*He takes out a pocket comb and mirror, and retires towards the dais to arrange his hair.*)

ELDER DANIELS: Oh, think of your immortal soul, man, not of your foolish face.

BLANCO: I can't change my soul, Elder: it changes me – sometimes Feemy: I'm too pale. Let me rub my cheek against yours, darling.

FEEMY: You lie: my colour's my own, such as it is. And a pretty colour you'll be when you're hung white and shot red.

BLANCO: Ain't she spiteful, Sheriff?

THE SHERIFF: Time's wasted on you. (*To Strapper.*) Go and see if the boys are ready. Some of them were short of cartridges, and went down to the store to buy them. They may as well have their fun; and it'll be shorter for him.

STRAPPER: Young Jack has brought a boxful up. They're all ready.

THE SHERIFF (*going to the dais and addressing Blanco*): Your place is at the bar there. Take it. (*Blanco bows ironically and goes to the bar.*) Miss Evans: you'd best sit at the table. (*She does so, at the corner nearest the bar. The Elder takes the opposite corner. The Sheriff takes his chair.*) All ready, Strapper.

STRAPPER (*at the door*): All in to begin.

The crowd comes in and fills the court. BABSY, JESSIE, *and* EMMA *come to the Sheriff's right;* HANNAH *and* LOTTIE *to his left.*

THE SHERIFF: Silence there. The jury will take their places as usual. (*They do so.*)

BLANCO: I challenge this jury, Sheriff.

THE FOREMAN: Do you, by Gosh?

THE SHERIFF: On what ground?

BLANCO: On the general ground that it's a rotten jury (*Laughter.*)

THE SHERIFF: That's not a lawful ground of challenge.

THE FOREMAN: It's a lawful ground for me to shoot yonder shunk at sight, first time I meet him, if he survives this trial.

BLANCO: I challenge the Foreman because he's prejudiced.

THE FOREMAN: I say you lie. We mean to hang you, Blanco Posnet; but you will be hanged fair.

THE JURY: Hear, hear!

STRAPPER (*to the Sheriff*): George: this is rot. How can you get an unprejudiced jury if the prisoner starts by telling them they're all rotten? If there's any prejudice against him he has himself to thank for it.

THE BOYS: That's so. Of course he has. Insulting the court! Challenge be jiggered! Gag him.

NESTOR (*a juryman with a long white beard, drunk, the oldest man present*): Besides, Sheriff, I go so far as to say that the man that is not prejudiced against a horse-thief is not fit to sit on a jury in this town.

THE BOYS: Right. Bully for you, Nestor! That's the straight truth. Of course he ain't. Hear, hear!

THE SHERIFF: That is no doubt true, old man. Still, you must get as unprejudiced as you can. The critter has a right to his chance, such as he is. So now go right ahead. If the prisoner don't like this jury, he should have stole a horse in another town; for this is all the jury he'll get here.

THE FOREMAN: That's so, Blanco Posnet.

THE SHERIFF (*to Blanco*): Don't you be uneasy. You will get justice here. It may be rough justice; but it is justice.

BLANCO: What is justice?

THE SHERIFF: Hanging horse-thieves is justice; so now you know. Now then: we've wasted enough time. Hustle with your witness there, will you?

BLANCO (*indignantly bringing down his fist on the bar*): Swear the jury. A rotten Sheriff you are not to know that the jury's got to be sworn.

THE FOREMAN (*called*): Be swore for you! Not likely. What do you say, old son?

NESTOR (*deliberately and solemnly*): I say: GUILTY!!!

THE BOYS (*tumultuously rushing at Blanco*): That's it. Guilty, guilty. Take him out and hang him. He's found guilty. Fetch a rope. Up with him. (*They are about to drag him from the bar.*)

THE SHERIFF (*rising, pistol in hand*): Hands off that man. Hands off him, I say, Squinty, or I drop you, and would if you were my own son. (*Dead silence.*) I'm Sheriff here; and it's for me to say when he may lawfully be hanged. (*They release him.*)

BLANCO: As the actor says in the play, 'a Daniel come to judgement'. Rotten actor he was, too.

THE SHERIFF: Elder Daniel is come to judgement all right, my lad. Elder: the floor is yours. (THE ELDER *rises.*) Give your evidence. The truth and the whole truth and nothing but the truth, so help you God.

ELDER DANIELS: Sheriff: let me off this. I didn't ought to swear away this man's life. He and I are, in a manner of speaking, brothers.

THE SHERIFF: It does you credit, Elder: every man here will acknowledge it. But religion is one thing: law is another. In religion we're all brothers. In law we cut our brother off when he steals horses.

THE FOREMAN: Besides, you needn't hang him, you know. There's plenty of willing hands to take that job off your conscience. So rip ahead, old son.

STRAPPER: You're accountable to me for the horse until you clear yourself, Elder: remember that.

BLANCO: Out with it, you fool.

ELDER DANIELS: You might own up, Blanco, as far as my evidence goes. Everybody knows I borrowed one of the Sheriff's horses from Strapper because my own's gone lame. Everybody knows you arrived in the town yesterday and put up in my house. Everybody knows that in the morning the horse was gone and you were gone.

BLANCO (*in a forensic manner*): Sheriff: the Elder, though known to you and to all here as no brother of mine and the rottenest liar in this town, is speaking the truth for the first time in his life as far as what he says about me is concerned. As to the horse, I say nothing; except that it was the rottenest horse you ever tried to sell.

THE SHERIFF: How do you know it was a rotten horse if you didn't steal it?

BLANCO: I don't know of my own knowledge. I only argue that if the horse had been worth its keep, you wouldn't have lent it to Strapper, and Strapper wouldn't have lent it to this eloquent and venerable ram. (*Suppressed laughter.*) And now I ask him this. (*To the Elder.*) Did we or did we not have a quarrel last evening about a certain article that was left by my mother, and that I considered I had a right to more than you? And did you say one word to me about the horse not belonging to you?

ELDER DANIELS: Why should I? We never said a word about the horse at all. How was I to know what it was in your mind to do?

BLANCO: Bear witness all that I had a right to take a horse from him without stealing to make up for what he denied me. I am no thief. But you haven't proved yet that I took the horse. Strapper Kemp: had I the horse when you took me or had I not?

STRAPPER: No, nor you hadn't a railway train neither. But Feemy Evans saw you pass on the horse at four o'clock twenty-five miles from the spot where I took you at seven on the road to Pony Harbor. Did you walk twenty-five miles in three hours? That so, Feemy? eh?

FEEMY: That's so. At four I saw him. (*To Blanco.*) That's done for you.

THE SHERIFF: You say you saw him on my horse?

FEEMY: I did.

BLANCO: And I ate it, I suppose, before Strapper fetched up with me. (*Suddenly and dramatically.*) Sheriff: I accuse Feemy of immoral relations with Strapper.

FEEMY: Oh you liar!

BLANCO: I accuse the fair Euphemia of immoral relations with every man in this town, including yourself, Sheriff. I say this is a conspiracy to kill me between Feemy and Strapper because I wouldn't touch Feemy with a pair of tongs. I say you daren't hang any white man on the word of a woman of bad character. I stand on the honour and virtue of my American manhood. I say that she's not had the oath, and that you daren't for the honour of the town give her the oath because her lips would blaspheme the holy Bible if they touched it. I say that's the law; and if you are a proper United States Sheriff and not a low-down lyncher, you'll hold up the law and not let it be dragged in the mud by your brother's kept woman.

Great excitement among the women. The men much puzzled.

JESSIE. That's right. She didn't ought to be let kiss the Book.

EMMA. How could the like of her tell the truth?

BABSY: It would be an insult to every respectable woman here to believe her.

FEEMY: It's easy to be respectable with nobody ever offering you a chance to be anything else.

THE WOMAN (*clamouring all together*): Shut up, you hussy. You're a disgrace. How dare you open your lips to answer your betters? Hold your tongue and learn your place, Miss. You painted slut! Whip her out of the town!

THE SHERIFF. Silence. Do you hear. Silence. (*The clamour ceases.*) Did anyone else see the prisoner with the horse?

FEEMY (*passionately*): Ain't I good enough?

BABSY: No. You're dirt: that's what you are.

FEEMY: And you —

THE SHERIFF: Silence. This trial is a man's job; and if the women forget their sex they can go out or be put out. Strapper and Miss Evans: you can't have it two ways. You can run straight, or you can run gay, so to speak; but you can't run both ways together. There is also a strong feeling among the men of this town that a line should be drawn between those that are straight wives and mothers and those that are, in the words of the Book of Books, taking the primrose path. We don't wish to be hard on any woman; and most of us have a personal regard for Miss Evans for the sake of old times; but there's no getting out of the fact that she has private reasons for wishing to oblige Strapper, and that – if she will excuse my saying so – she is not what I might call morally particular as to what she does to oblige him. Therefore I ask the prisoner not to drive us to give Miss Evans the oath. I ask him to tell us fair and square, as a man who has but a few minutes between him and eternity, what he done with my horse.

THE BOYS: Hear, hear! That's right. That's fair. That does it. Now, Blanco. Own up.

BLANCO: Sheriff: you touch me home. This is a rotten world; but there is still one thing in it that remains sacred even to the rottenest of us, and that is a horse.

THE BOYS: Good. Well said, Blanco. That's straight.

BLANCO: You have a right to your horse, Sheriff; and if I could put you in the way of getting it back, I would. But if I had that horse I shouldn't be here. As I hope to be saved, Sheriff – or rather as I hope to be damned; for I have no taste for pious company and no talent for playing the harp – I know no more of that horse's whereabouts than you do yourself.

STRAPPER: Who did you trade him to?

BLANCO: I did not trade him. I got nothing for him or by him. I stand here with a rope round my neck for the want of him. When you took me, did I fight like a thief or run like a thief; and was there any sign of a horse on me or near me?

STRAPPER: You were looking at a rainbow like a damned silly fool instead of keeping your wits about you; and we stole up on you and had you tight before you could draw a bead on us.

THE SHERIFF: That don't sound like good sense. What would he look at a rainbow for?

BLANCO: I'll tell you, Sheriff. I was looking at it because there was something written on it.

SHERIFF: How do you mean written on it.

BLANCO: The words were, 'I've got the cinch on you this time, Blanco Posnet.' Yes, Sheriff, I saw those words in green on the red streak of the rainbow; and as I saw them I felt Strapper's grab on my arm and Squinty's on my pistol.

THE FOREMAN: He's shammin' mad: that's what he is. Ain't it about time to give a verdict and have a bit of fun, Sheriff?

THE BOYS: Yes, let's have a verdict. We're wasting the whole afternoon. Cut it short.

THE SHERIFF (*making up his mind*): Swear Feemy. Evans, Elder. She don't need to touch the Book. Let her say the words.

FEEMY: Worse people than me has kissed that Book. What wrong I've done, most of you went shares in. I've to live, haven't I? same as the rest of you. However, it makes no odds to me, I guess the truth is the truth and a lie is a lie, on the Book or off it.

BABSY: Do as you're told. Who are you, to be let talk about it?

THE SHERIFF: Silence there, I tell you. Sail ahead, Elder.

ELDER DANIELS: Feemy Evans: do you swear to tell the truth and the whole truth and nothing but the truth, so help you God.

FEEMY: I do, so help me —

SHERIFF: That's enough. Now, on your oath, did you see the prisoner on my horse this morning on the road to Pony Harror?

FEEMY: On my oath — (*Disturbance and crowding at the door.*)

AT THE DOOR: Now then, now then! Where are you shovin' to? What's up? Order in court. Chuck him out. Silence. You can't come in here. Keep back.

STRAPPER *rushes to the door and forces his way out.*

SHERIFF (*savagely*): What's this noise? Can't you keep quiet there? Is this a Sheriff's court or is it a saloon?

BLANCO: Don't interrupt a lady in the act of hanging a gentleman. Where's your manners?

FEEMY: I'll hang you, Blanco Posnet. I will. I wouldn't for fifty dollars I hadn't seen you this morning. I'll teach you to be civil to me next time, for all I'm not good enough to kiss the Book.

BLANCO: Lord keep me wicked till I die! I'm game for anything while you're spitting dirt at me, Feemy.

RENEWED TUMULT AT THE DOOR: Here, what's this? Fire them out. Not me. Who are you that I should get out of your

way? Oh, stow it. Well, she can't come in. What woman?
What horse? What's the good of shoving like that? Who says?
No! you don't say!

THE SHERIFF: Gentlemen of the Vigilance Committee: clear
that doorway. Out with them in the name of the law.

STRAPPER (*without*): Hold hard, George. (*At the door.*) They've
got the horse. (*He comes in, followed by* WAGGONER JO, *an
elderly carter, who crosses the court to the jury side.* STRAPPER *pushes
his way to the Sheriff and speaks privately to him.*)

THE BOYS: What! No! Got the horse! Sheriff's horse! Who took
it, then? Where? Get out. Yes it is, sure. I tell you it is. It's the
horse all right enough. Rot. Go and look. By Gum!

THE SHERIFF (*to Strapper*): You don't say!

STRAPPER: It's here, I tell you.

WAGGONER JO: It's here all right enough, Sheriff.

STRAPPER: And they've got the thief too.

ELDER DANIELS: Then it ain't Blanco.

STRAPPER: No: it's a woman. (BLANCO *yells and covers his eyes
with his hands.*)

THE WHOLE CROWD: A woman!

THE SHERIFF: Well, fetch her in. (STRAPPER *goes out. The
Sheriff continues, to Feemy.*) And what do you mean, you lying
jade, by putting up this story on us about Blanco?

FEEMY: I ain't put up no story on you. This is a plant: you see if
it isn't.

STRAPPER *returns with a woman. Her expression of intense grief
silences them as they crane over one another's heads to see her.* STRAP-
PER *takes her to the corner of the table.* THE ELDER *moves up to
make room for her.*

BLANCO (*terrified*): Sheriff: that woman ain't real. You take care.
That woman will make you do what you never intended. That's
the rainbow woman. That's the woman that brought me to
this.

THE SHERIFF: Shut your mouth, will you? You've got the
horrors. (*To the woman.*) Now you. Who are you? and what are
you doing with a horse that doesn't belong to you?

THE WOMAN: I took it to save my child's life. I thought it would get me to a doctor in time. The child was choking with croup.

BLANCO (*strangling, and trying to laugh*): A little choker: that's the word for him. His choking wasn't real: wait and see mine. (*He feels his neck with a sob.*)

THE SHERIFF: Where's the child?

STRAPPER: On Pug Jackson's bench in his shed. He's makin' a coffin for it.

BLANCO (*with a horrible convulsion of the throat – frantically*): Dead! The little Judas kid! The child I gave my life for! (*He breaks into hideous laughter.*)

THE SHERIFF (*jarred beyond endurance by the sound*): Hold your noise, will you? Shove his neckerchief into his mouth if he don't stop. (*To the woman.*) Don't you mind him, maam: he's mad with drink and devilment. I suppose there's no fake about this, Strapper. Who found her?

WAGGONER JO: I did, Sheriff. There's no fake about it. I came on her on the track round by Red Mountain. She was settin' on the ground with the dead body on her lap, stupid-like. The horse was grazin' on the other side o' the road.

THE SHERIFF (*puzzled*): Well, this is blamed queer. (*To the woman.*) What call had you to take the horse from Elder Daniels's stable to find a doctor? There's a doctor in the very next house.

BLANCO (*mopping his dabbled red crest and trying to be ironically gay*): Story simply won't wash, my angel. You got it from the man that stole the horse. He gave it to you because he was a softy and went to bits when you played off the sick kid on him. Well, I guess that clears me. I'm not that sort. Catch me putting my neck in a noose for anybody's kid!

THE FOREMAN: Don't you go putting her up to what to say. She said she took it.

THE WOMAN: Yes: I took it from a man that met me. I thought God sent him to me. I rode here joyfully thinking so all the time to myself. Then I noticed that the child was like lead in my arms. God would never have been so cruel as to send me the horse to disappoint me like that.

BLANCO: Just what He would do.

STRAPPER: We ain't got nothin' to do with that. This is the man, ain't he? (*Pointing to Blanco.*)

THE WOMAN (*pulling herself together after looking scaredly at Blanco, and then at the Sheriff and at the jury*): No.

THE FOREMAN: You lie.

THE SHERIFF: You've got to tell us the truth. That's the law, you know.

THE WOMAN: The man looked a bad man. He cursed me; and he cursed the child: God forgive him! But something came over him. I was desperate. I put the child in his arms; and it got its little fingers down his neck and called him Daddy and tried to kiss him; for it was not right in its head with the fever. He said it was a little Judas kid, and that it was betraying him with a kiss, and that he'd swing for it. And then he gave me the horse, and went away crying and laughing and singing dreadful dirty wicked words to hymn tunes like as if he had seven devils in him.

STRAPPER: She's lying. Give her the oath, George.

THE SHERIFF: Go easy there. You're a smart boy, Strapper; but you're not Sheriff yet. This is my job. You just wait. I submit that we're in a difficulty here. If Blanco was the man, the lady can't, as a white woman, give him away. She oughtn't to be put in the position of having either to give him away or commit perjury. On the other hand, we don't want a horse-thief to get off through a lady's delicacy.

THE FOREMAN: No we don't; and we don't intend he shall. Not while I am foreman of this jury.

BLANCO (*with intense expression*): A rotten foreman! Oh, what a rotten foreman!

THE SHERIFF: Shut up, will you? Providence shows us a way out here. Two women saw Blanco with a horse. One has a delicacy about saying so. The other will excuse me saying that delicacy is not her strongest holt. She can give the necessary

D

witness. Feemy Evans: you've taken the oath. You saw the man that took the horse.

FEEMY: I did. And he was a low-down rotten drunken lying hound that would go further to hurt a woman any day than to help her. And if he ever did a good action it was because he was too drunk to know what he was doing. So it's no harm to hang him. She said he cursed her and went away blaspheming and singing things that were not fit for the child to hear.

BLANCO (*troubled*): I didn't mean them for the child to hear, you venomous devil.

THE SHERIFF: All that's got nothing to do with us. The question you have to answer is, was that man Blanco Posnet?

THE WOMAN: No. I say no. I swear it. Sheriff: don't hang that man: oh don't. You may hang me instead if you like: I've nothing to live for now. You daren't take her word against mine. She never had a child: I can see it in her face.

FEEMY (*stung to the quick*): I can hang him in spite of you, anyhow. Much good your child is to you now, lying there on Pug Jackson's bench!

BLANCO (*rushing at her with a shriek*): I'll twist your heart out of you for that. (*They seize him before he can reach her.*)

FEEMY (*mocking him as he struggles to get at her*): Ha, ha, Blanco Posnet. You can't touch me; and I can hang you. Ha, ha! Oh, I'll do for you. I'll twist your heart and I'll twist your neck. (*He is dragged back to the bar and leans on it, gasping and exhausted.*) Give me the oath again, Elder. I'll settle him. And do you (*To the woman.*) take you sickly face away from in front of me.

STRAPPER: Just turn your back on her there, will you?

THE WOMAN: God knows I don't want to see her commit murder. (*She folds her shawl over her head.*)

THE SHERIFF: Now, Miss Evans: cut it short. Was the prisoner the man you saw this morning or was he not? Yes or no?

FEEMY (*a little hysterically*): I'll tell you fast enough. Don't think I'm a softy.

THE SHERIFF (*losing patience*): Here: we've had enough of this.

You tell the truth, Feemy Evans; and let us have no more of your lip. Was the prisoner the man or was he not? On your oath?

FEEMY: On my oath and as I'm a living woman — (*flinching.*) Oh God! he felt the little child's hands on his neck – I can't (*Bursting into a flood of tears and scolding at the other woman.*) It's you with your snivelling face that has put me off it. (*Desperately.*) No: it wasn't him. I only said it out of spite because he insulted me. May I be struck dead if I ever saw him with the horse! *Everybody draws a long breath. Dead silence.*

BLANCO (*whispering at her*): Softy! Cry-baby! Landed like me! Doing what you never intended! (*Taking up his hat and speaking in his ordinary tone.*) I presume I may go now, Sheriff.

STRAPPER: Here, hold hard.

THE FOREMAN: Not if we know it, you don't.

THE BOYS (*barring the way to the door*): You stay where you are. Stop a bit, stop a bit. Don't you be in such a hurry. Don't let him go. Not much.

BLANCO *stands motionless, his eye fixed, thinking hard, and apparently deaf to what is going on.*

THE SHERIFF (*rising solemnly*): Silence there. Wait a bit. I take it that if the Sheriff is satisfied and the owner of the horse is satisfied, there's no more to be said. I have had to remark on former occasions that what is wrong with this court is that there's too many Sheriffs in it. Today there is going to be one, and only one; and that one is your humble servant. I call that to the notice of the Foreman of the jury, and also to the notice of young Strapper. I am also the owner of the horse. Does any man say I am not? (*Silence.*) Very well, then. In my opinion, to commandeer a horse for the purpose of getting a dying child to a doctor is not stealing, provided, as in the present case, that the horse is returned safe and sound. I rule that there has been no theft.

NESTOR: That ain't the law.

THE SHERIFF: I fine you a dollar for contempt of court, and will collect it myself off you as you leave the building. And as the boys have been disappointed of their natural sport, I shall give them a little fun by standing outside the door and taking up a collection for the bereaved mother of the late kid that showed up Blanco Posnet.

THE BOYS: A collection. Oh, I say! Calls that sport? Is this a mothers' meeting? Well, I'll be jiggered! Where does the sport come in?

THE SHERIFF (*continuing*): The sport comes in, my friends, not so much in contributing as in seeing others fork out. Thus each contributes to the general enjoyment; and all contribute to his. Blanco Posnet: you go free under the protection of the Vigilance Committee for just long enough to get you out of this town, which is not a healthy place for you. As you are in a hurry, I'll sell you the horse at a reasonable figure. Now, boys, let nobody go out till I get to the door. The court is adjourned. (*He goes out.*)

STRAPPER (*to* FEEMY, *as he goes to the door*): I'm done with you. Do you hear? I'm done with you. (*He goes out sulkily.*)

FEEMY (*calling after him*): As if I cared about a stingy brat like you! Go back to the freckled maypole you left for me: you've been fretting for her long enough.

THE FOREMAN (*to* BLANCO, *on his way out*): A man like you makes me sick. Just sick. (BLANCO *makes no sign. The* FOREMAN *spits disgustedly, and follows* STRAPPER *out. The* JURYMEN *leave the box, except* NESTOR, *who collapses in a drunken sleep.*)

BLANCO (*suddenly rushing from the bar to the table and jumping up on it*): Boys, I'm going to preach you a sermon on the moral of this day's proceedings.

THE BOYS (*crowding round him*): Yes: let's have a sermon. Go ahead, Blanco. Silence for Elder Blanco. Tune the organ. Let us pray.

NESTOR (*staggering out of his sleep*): Never hold up your head in this town again. I'm done with you.

BLANCO (*pointing inexorably to Nestor*): Drunk in church. Disturbing the preacher. Hand him out.

THE BOYS (*chivying Nestor out*): Now, Nestor, outside. Outside,

Nestor. Out you go. Get your subscription ready for the Sheriff. Skiddoo, Nestor.

NESTOR: Afraid to be hanged! Afraid to be hanged! (*At the door.*) Coward! (*He is thrown out.*)

BLANCO: Dearly beloved brethren —

A BOY: Same to you, Blanco. (*Laughter.*)

BLANCO: And many of them. Boys: this is a rotten world.

ANOTHER BOY: Lord have mercy on us' miserable sinners. (*More laughter.*)

BLANCO (*forcibly*): No: that's where you're wrong. Don't flatter yourselves that you're miserable sinners. Am I a miserable sinner? No: I'm a fraud and a failure. I started in to be a bad man like the rest of you. You all started in to be bad men or you wouldn't be in this jumped-up, jerked-off, hospital-turned-out camp that calls itself a town. I took the broad path because I thought I was a man and not a snivelling canting turning-the-other-cheek apprentice angel serving his time in a vale of tears. They talked Christianity to us on Sundays; but when they really meant business they told us never to take a blow without giving it back, and to get dollars. When they talked the golden rule to me, I just looked at them as if they weren't there, and spat. But when they told me to try to live my life so that I could always look my fellow-man straight in the eye and tell him to go to hell, that fetched me.

THE BOYS: Quite right. Good. Bully for you, Blanco, old son. Right good sense too. Aha-a-ah!

BLANCO: Yes; but what's come of it all? Am I a real bad man? a man of game and grit? a man that does what he likes and goes over or through other people to his own gain? or am I a snivelling cry-baby that let a horse his life depended on be took from him by a woman, and then sat on the grass looking at the rainbow and let himself be took like a hare in a trap by Strapper Kemp: a lad whose back I or any grown man here could break against his knee? I'm a rottener fraud and failure than the Elder here. And you're all as rotten as me, or you'd have lynched me.

A BOY: Anything to oblige you, Blanco.

ANOTHER: We can do it yet if you feel really bad about it.

BLANCO: No: the devil's gone out of you. We're all frauds.
There's none of us real good and none of us real bad.

ELDER DANIELS: There is One above, Blanco.

BLANCO: What do you know about Him? you that always talk as
if He never did anything without asking your rotten leave
first? Why did the child die? Tell me that if you can. He can't
have wanted to kill the child. Why did He make me go soft on
the child if He was going hard on it Himself? Why should He
go hard on the innocent kid and go soft on a rotten thing like
me? Why did I go soft myself? Why did the Sheriff go soft?
Why did Feemy go soft? What's this game that upsets our
game? For seems to me there's two games bein' played. Our
game is a rotten game that makes me feel I'm dirt and that
you're all as rotten dirt as me. T'other game may be a silly
game; but it ain't rotten. When the Sheriff played it he stopped
being rotten. When Feemy played it the paint nearly dropped
off her face. When I played it I cursed myself for a fool; but I
lost the rotten feel all the same.

ELDER DANIELS: It was the Lord speaking to your soul,
Blanco.

BLANCO: Oh yes: you know all about the Lord, don't you?
You're in the Lord's confidence. He wouldn't for the world do
anything to shock you, would He, Boozy dear? Yah! What
about the croup? It was early days when He made the croup, I
guess. It was the best He could think of then; but when it
turned out wrong on His hands He made you and me to fight
the croup for Him. You bet He didn't make us for nothing; and
He wouldn't have made us at all if He could have done His
work without us. By Gum, that must be what we're for! He'd
never have made us to be rotten drunken blackguards like me,
and good-for-nothing rips like Feemy. He made me because He
had a job for me. He let me run loose 'til the job was ready; and
then I had to come along and do it, hanging or no hanging.
And I tell you it didn't feel rotten: it felt bully, just bully. Any-

how, I got the rotten feel off me for a minute of my life; and I'll go through fire to get it off me again. Look here! which of you will marry Feemy Evans?

THE BOYS (*uproariously*): Who speaks first? Who'll marry Feemy? Come along, Jack. Now's your chance, Peter. Pass along a husband for Feemy. Oh my! Feemy!

FEEMY (*shortly*): Keep your tongue off me, will you?

BLANCO: Feemy was a rose of the broad path, wasn't she? You all thought her the champion bad woman of this district. Well, she's a failure as a bad woman; and I'm a failure as a bad man. So let Brother Daniels marry us to keep all the rottenness in the family. What do you say, Feemy?

FEEMY: Thank you; but when I marry I'll marry a man that could do a decent action without surprising himself out of his senses. You're like a child with a new toy: you and your bit of human kindness!

THE WOMAN: How many would have done it with their life at stake?

FEEMY: Oh well, if you're so much taken with him, marry him yourself. You'd be what people call a good wife to him, wouldn't you?

THE WOMAN: I was a good wife to the child's father. I don't think any woman wants to be a good wife twice in her life. I want somebody to be a good husband to me now.

BLANCO: Any offer, gentlemen, on that understanding? (*The boys shake their heads.*) Oh, it's a rotten game, our game. Here's a real good woman; and she's had enough of it, finding that it only led to being put upon.

HANNAH: Well, if there was nothing wrong in the world there wouldn't be anything left for us to do, would there?

ELDER DANIELS: Be of good cheer, brothers. Seek the path.

BLANCO: No. No more paths. No more broad and narrow. No more good and bad. There's no good and bad; but by Jiminy, gents, there's a rotten game, and there's a great game. I played the rotten game; but the great game was played on me; and now I'm for the great game every time. Amen. Gentlemen: let us adjourn to the saloon. I stand the drinks. (*He jumps down from the table.*)

THE BOYS: Right you are, Blanco. Drinks round. Come along, boys. Blanco's standing. Right along to the Elder's. Hurrah! (*They rush out, dragging the Elder with them.*)

BLANCO (*to Feemy, offering his hand*): Shake, Feemy.

FEEMY: Get along, you blackguard.

BLANCO: It's come over me again, same as when the kid touched me, same as when you swore a lie to save my neck.

FEEMY: Oh well, here. (*They shake hands.*)

The Glimpse of Reality

A Tragedietta

I see plenty of good in the world working itself out as fast as the idealist will allow it; and if they would only let it alone and learn to respect reality we should all get along much better and faster.

CHARACTERS

COUNT FERRUCCIO (*at first disguised as* THE FRIAR)
SQUARCIO, *an Innkeeper*
GIULIA, *his daughter, betrothed to*
SANDRO, *a young Fisherman*

SCENE: The exterior of an inn on the edge of an Italian lake. Evening – twilight.

PERIOD: Fifteenth century.

The play was first performed in London at the Arts Theatre Club on 20 November 1907.

THE GLIMPSE OF REALITY

In 1926 Shaw decided to publish a volume of a few short pieces he had written at various times. These appeared under the title of *Translations and Tomfooleries*. There was, in fact, only one translation; the rest were what he termed 'trifles and tomfooleries'. Of these *The Glimpse of Reality* which he described as a 'tragedietta' was the only 'trifle'; the other pieces were all 'tomfooleries'.

Shaw considered these little playlets to have the same relationship to the main body of his work that a great composer's little piano pieces for instance, bore to his symphonies.

However he was careful to make it clear that he did not mean by 'trifles and tomfooleries' that 'their words are utterly void of wit and wisdom, or their figures characterless; for this kind of work would be unbearable if it added deficiency to folly . . . They may disgust the admirers of my more pretentious work; but these highbrows must remember that there is a demand for little things as well as for big things, and as I happen to have a few little things in my shop I may as well put them in the window with the rest'. Incidentally the publication of these pieces in book form is a reminder that many of Shaw's early plays were published to be *read* as much as to be acted; this explains why it is that he adds such detailed descriptions of settings, stage directions and characters in the plays.

The Glimpse of Reality reads rather like a good dramatization of a medieval fabliau (or tale); it has the typical characters of a fabliau: a sinister nobleman, simple peasants and a cunning friar (though in Shaw's play the friar is also the nobleman in disguise). The play presents no particular difficulties either in setting or in acting. Young people should be able to put it over effectively.

THE GLIMPSE OF REALITY

In the fifteenth century A.D. Gloaming. An inn on the edge of an Italian lake. A stone cross with a pedestal of steps. A very old friar sitting on the steps. The angelus rings. THE FRIAR *prays and crosses himself. A girl ferries a boat to the shore and comes up the bank to the cross.*

THE GIRL: Father: were you sent here by a boy from —

THE FRIAR (*in a high, piping, but clear voice*): I'm a very old man. Oh, very old. Old enough to be your great grandfather, my daughter. Oh, very very old.

THE GIRL: But were you sent here by a boy from —

THE FRIAR: Oh yes, yes, yes, yes, yes. Quite a boy, he was. Very young. And I'm very old. Oh, very very old, dear daughter.

THE GIRL: Are you a holy man?

THE FRIAR (*ecstatically*): Oh, very holy. Very, very, very, very holy.

THE GIRL: But have you your wits still about you, father? Can you absolve me from a great sin?

THE FRIAR: Oh yes, yes, yes. A very great sin. I'm very old; but I've my wits about me. I'm one hundred and thirteen years old, by the grace of Our Lady; but I still remember all my Latin; and I can bind and loose; and I'm very very wise; for I'm old and have left far behind me the world, the flesh, and the devil. You see I am blind, daughter; but when a boy told me that there was a duty for me to do here, I came without a guide, straight to this spot, led by St Barbara. She led me to this stone, daughter. It's a comfortable stone to me: she has blessed it for me.

THE GIRL: It's a cross, Father.

THE FRIAR (*piping rapturously*): Oh blessed, blessed, ever blessed be my holy patroness for leading me to this sacred spot. Is there any building near this, daughter? The boy mentioned an inn.

THE GIRL: There is an inn, Father, not twenty yards away. It's kept by my father, Squarcio.

THE FRIAR: And is there a barn where a very very old man may sleep and have a handful of peas for his supper?

THE GIRL: There is bed and board both for holy men who will take the guilt of our sins from us. Swear to me on the cross that you are a very holy man.

THE FRIAR: I'll do better than that, daughter. I'll prove my holiness to you by a miracle.

THE GIRL: A miracle!

THE FRIAR: A most miraculous miracle. A wonderful miracle! When I was only eighteen years of age I was already famous for my devoutness. When the hand of the blessed Saint Barbara, which was chopped off in the days when the church was persecuted, was found at Viterbo, I was selected by the Pope himself to carry it to Rome for that blessed lady's festival there; and since that my hand has never grown old. It remains young and warm and plump whilst the rest of my body is withered almost to dust, and my voice is cracked and become the whistling you now hear.

THE GIRL: Is that true? Let me see. (*He takes her hand in his. She kneels and kisses it fervently.*) Oh, it's true. You are a saint. Heaven has sent you in answer to my prayer.

THE FRIAR: As soft as your neck, is it not? (*He caresses her neck.*)

THE GIRL: It thrills me: it is wonderful.

THE FRIAR: It thrills me also, daughter. That, too, is a miracle at my age.

THE GIRL: Father —

THE FRIAR: Come closer, daughter. I'm very very old and very very very deaf: you must speak quite close to my ear if you speak low. (*She kneels with her breast against his arm and her chin on his shoulder*.) Good. Good. That's better. Oh, I'm very very old.

THE GIRL: Father: I am about to commit a deadly sin.

THE FRIAR: Do, my daughter. Do, do, do, do, do.

THE GIRL (*discouraged*): Oh, you do not hear what I say.

THE FRIAR: Not hear! Then come closer, daughter. Oh, much, much closer. Put your arm round my shoulders, and speak in my ear. Do not be ashamed, my daughter: I'm only a sack of old bones. You can hear them rattle. (*He shakes his shoulders and makes the beads of his rosary rattle at the same time*.) Listen to the old man's bones rattling. Oh, take the old old man to heaven, Blessed Barbara.

THE GIRL: Your wits are wandering. Listen to me. Are you listening?

THE FRIAR: Yes yes yes yes yes yes yes. Remember: whether I hear or not, I can absolve. All the better for you perhaps if I do not hear the worst. He! He! He! Well well. When my wits wander, squeeze my young hand; and the blessed Barbara will restore my faculties. (*She squeezes his hand vigorously*.) That's right. Tha-a-a-a-at's right. Now I remember what I am and who you are. Proceed, my child.

THE GIRL: Father, I am to be married this year to a young fisherman.

THE FRIAR: The devil you are, my dear.

THE GIRL (*squeezing his hand*): Oh listen, listen; you are wandering again.

THE FRIAR: That's right: hold my hand tightly. I understand, I understand. This young fisherman is neither very beautiful nor very brave; but he is honest and devoted to you; and there is something about him different to all the other young men.

THE GIRL: You know him, then!

THE FRIAR: No no no no no. I'm too old to remember people. But Saint Barbara tells me everything.

THE GIRL: Then you know why we can't marry yet.

THE FRIAR: He is too poor. His mother will not let him unless his bride has a dowry —

THE GIRL (*interrupting him impetuously*): Yes, yes: oh blessed be Saint Barbara for sending you to me! Thirty crowns – thirty crowns from a poor girl like me: it is wicked – monstrous. I must sin to earn it.

THE FRIAR: That will not be your sin, but his mother's.

THE GIRL: Oh, that is true: I never thought of that. But will she suffer for it?

THE FRIAR: Thousands of years in purgatory for it, my daughter. The worse the sin, the longer she will suffer. So let her have it as hot as possible. (*The girl recoils.*) Do not let go my hand: I'm wandering. (*She squeezes his hand.*) That's right, darling. Sin is a very wicked thing, my daughter. Even a mother-in-law's sin is very expensive; for your husband would stint you to pay for masses for her soul.

THE GIRL: That is true. You are very wise, Father.

THE FRIAR: Let it be a venial sin: an amiable sin. What sin were you thinking of, for instance?

THE GIRL: There is a young Count Ferruccio (*The Friar starts at the name,*) son of the tyrant of Parma —

THE FRIAR: An excellent young man, daughter. You could not sin with a more excellent young man. But thirty crowns is too much to ask from him. He can't afford it. He is a beggar: an outcast. He made love to Madonna Brigita, the sister of Cardinal Poldi, a Cardinal eighteen years of age, a nephew of the Holy Father. The Cardinal surprised Ferruccio with his sister; and Ferruccio's temper got the better of him. He threw that holy young Cardinal out of the window and broke his arm.

THE GIRL: You know everything.

THE FRIAR: Saint Barbara, my daughter, Saint Barbara. *I* know nothing. But where have you seen Ferruccio? Saint Barbara says that he never saw you in his life, and has not thirty crowns in the world.

THE GIRL: Oh, why does not Saint Barbara tell you that I am an honest girl who would not sell herself for a thousand crowns.

THE FRIAR: Do not give way to pride, daughter. Pride is one of the seven deadly sins.

THE GIRL: I know that, Father; and believe me, I'm humble and good. I swear to you by Our Lady that it is not Ferruccio's love that I must take, but his life. (*The Friar, startled, turns powerfully on her.*) Do not be angry, dear Father: do not cast me off. What is a poor girl to do? We are very poor, my father and I. And I am not to kill him. I am only to decoy him here; for he is a devil for women; and once he is in the inn, my father will do the rest.

THE FRIAR (*in a rich baritone voice*): Will he, by thunder and lightning and the flood and all the saints, will he? (*He flings off his gown and beard, revealing himself as a handsome youth, a nobleman by his dress, as he springs up and rushes to the door of the inn, which he batters with a stone.*) Ho there, Squarcio, rascal, assassin, son of a pig: come out that I may break every bone in your carcass.

THE GIRL: You are a young man!

THE FRIAR: Another miracle of Saint Barbara. (*Kicking the door.*) Come out, whelp: come out, rat. Come out and be killed. Come out and be beaten to a jelly. Come out, dog, swine, animal, mangy hound, lousy — (SQUARCIO *comes out, sword in hand.*) Do you know who I am, dog?

SQUARCIO (*impressed*): No, your excellency.

THE FRIAR: I am Ferruccio, Count Ferruccio, the man you are to kill, the man your devil of a daughter is to decoy, the man who is now going to cut you into forty thousand pieces and throw you into the lake.

SQUARCIO: Keep your temper, Signor Count.

FERRUCCIO: I'll not keep my temper. I've an uncontrollable temper. I got blinding splitting headaches if I do not relieve my temper by acts of violence. I'll relieve it now by pounding you to jelly, assassin that you are.

SQUARCIO (*shrugging his shoulders*): As you please, Signor Count. I may as well earn my money now as another time. (*He handles his sword.*)

FERRUCCIO: Ass: do you suppose I have trusted myself in this territory without precautions? My father has made a wager with your feudal lord here about me.

SQUARCIO: What wager, may it please your excellency?

FERRUCCIO: What wager, blockhead! Why, that if I am assassinated, the murderer will not be brought to justice.

SQUARCIO: So that if I kill you —

FERRUCCIO: Your Baron will lose ten crowns unless you are broken on the wheel for it.

SQUARCIO: Only ten crowns, Excellency! Your father does not value your life very highly.

FERRUCCIO: Dolt. Can you not reason? If the sum were larger your Baron would win it by killing me himself and breaking somebody else on the wheel for it: you, most likely. Ten crowns is just enough to make him break you on the wheel if you kill me, but not enough to pay for all the masses that would have to be said for him if the guilt were his.

SQUARCIO: That is very clever, Excellency. (*Sheathing his sword.*) You shall not be slain: I will take care of that. If anything happens, it will be an accident.

FERRUCCIO: Body of Bacchus! I forgot that trick. I should have killed you when my blood was hot.

SQUARCIO: Will your Excellency please to step in. My best room and my best cooking are at your Excellency's disposal.

FERRUCCIO: To the devil with your mangy kennel! You want to tell every traveller that Count Ferruccio slept in your best bed and was eaten by your army of fleas. Take yourself out of my sight when you have told me where the next inn is.

SQUARCIO: I'm sorry to thwart your Excellency; but I have not forgotten your father's wager; and until you leave this terri- I shall stick to you like your shadow.

FERRUCCIO: And why, pray?

SQUARCIO: Someone else might kill your Excellency; and, as you say, my illustrious Baron might break me on the wheel for your father's ten crowns. I must protect your Excellency whether your Excellency is willing or not.

FERRUCCIO: If you dare to annoy me, I'll handle your bones so that there will be nothing left for the hangman to break. Now what do you say?

SQUARCIO: I say that your Excellency over-rates your Excellency's strength. You would have no more chance against me than a grasshopper. (FERRUCCIO *makes a demonstration.*) Oh, I know that your Excellency has been taught by fencers and wrestlers and the like; but I can take all you can give me without turning a hair, and settle the account when you are out of breath. That is why common men are dangerous, your Excellency: they are inured to toil and endurance. Besides, I know all the tricks.

THE GIRL: Do not attempt to quarrel with my father, Count. It must be as he says. It is his profession to kill. What could you do against him? If you want to beat somebody, you must beat me. (*She goes into the inn.*)

SQUARCIO: I advise you not to try that, Excellency. She also is very strong.

FERRUCCIO: Then I shall have a headache: that's all. (*He throws himself ill-humouredly on a bench at the table outside the inn. GIULIA returns with a tablecloth and begins preparing the table for a meal.*)

SQUARCIO: A good supper, Excellency, will prevent that. And Giulia will sing for you.

FERRUCCIO: Not while there's a broomstick in the house to break her ugly head with. Do you suppose I'm going to listen to the howling of a she-wolf who wanted me to absolve her for getting me killed?

SQUARCIO: The poor must live as well as the rich, sir. Giulia is a good girl. (*He goes into the inn.*)

FERRUCCIO (*shouting after him*): Must the rich die that the poor may live?

GIULIA: The poor often die that the rich may live.

FERRUCCIO: What an honour for them! But it would have been no honour for me to die merely that you might marry your clod of a fisherman.

GIULIA: You are spiteful, Signor.

FERRUCCIO: I am no troubadour, Giuliaccia, if that is what you mean.

GIULIA: How did you know about my Sandro and his mother? How were you so wise when you pretended to be an old friar? you that are so childish now that you are yourself!

FERRUCCIO: I take it that either Saint Barbara inspired me, or else that you are a great fool.

GIULIA: Saint Barbara will surely punish you for that wicked lie you told about her hand.

FERRUCCIO: The hand that thrilled you?

GIULIA: That was blasphemy. You should not have done it. You made me feel as if I had had a taste of heaven; and then you poisoned it in my heart as a taste of hell. That was wicked and cruel. You nobles are cruel.

FERRUCCIO: Well! do you expect us to nurse your babies for you? Our work is to rule and to fight. Ruling is nothing but inflicting cruelties on wrongdoers: fighting is nothing but being cruel to one's enemies. You poor people leave us all the cruel work, and then wonder that we are cruel. Where would you be if we left it undone? Outside the life I lead all to myself – the life of thought and poetry – I know only two pleasures: cruelty and lust. I desire revenge: I desire women. And both of them disappoint me when I get them.

GIULIA: It would have been a good deed to kill you, I think.

FERRUCCIO: Killing is always sport, my Giuliaccia.

SANDRO'S VOICE (on the lake): Giulietta! Giulietta!

FERRUCCIO (calling to him): Stop that noise. Your Giulietta is here with a young nobleman. Come up and amuse him. (To Giulietta.) What will you give me if I tempt him to defy his mother and marry you without a dowry?

GIULIA: You are tempting me. A poor girl can give no more than she has. I should think you were a devil if you were not a noble, which is worse. (She goes out to meet Sandro.)

FERRUCCIO (calling after her): The devil does evil for pure love of it: he does not ask a price: he offers it. (SQUARCIO returns.) Prepare supper for four, bandit.

SQUARCIO: Is your appetite so great in this heat, Signor?

FERRUCCIO: There will be four to supper. You, I, your daughter,

and Sandro. Do not stint yourselves: I pay for all. Go and prepare more food.

SQUARCIO: Your order is already obeyed, Excellency.

FERRUCCIO: How?

SQUARCIO: I prepared for four, having you here to pay. The
only difference your graciousness makes is that we shall have
the honour to eat with you instead of after you.

FERRUCCIO: Dog of a bandit: you should have been born a
nobleman.

SQUARCIO: I was born noble, signor; but as we had no money to
maintain our pretensions, I dropped them. (*He goes back into the
inn.*)

Giulia returns with Sandro.

GIULIA: This is the lad, Excellency. Sandro: this is his lordship
Count Ferruccio.

SANDRO: At your lordship's service.

FERRUCCIO: Sit down, Sandro. You, Giulia, and Squarcio are
my guests. (*They sit*).

GIULIA: I've told Sandro everything, Excellency.

FERRUCCIO: And what does Sandro say? (SQUARCIO *returns
with a tray.*)

GIULIA: He says that if you have ten crowns in your purse, and
we kill you, we can give them to the Baron. It would be the
same to him as if he got it from your illustrious father.

SQUARCIO: Stupid: the Count is cleverer than you think. No
matter how much money you give the Baron he can always get
ten crowns more by breaking me on the wheel if the Count is
killed.

GIULIA: That is true. Sandro did not think of that.

SANDRO (*with cheerful politeness*): Oh! what a head I have! I am not
clever, Excellency. At the same time you must know that I did
not mean my Giulietta to tell you. I know my duty to your
Excellency better than that.

FERRUCIO: Come! You are dear people: charming people. Let
us get to work at the supper. You shall be the mother of
the family and give us our portions, Giulietta. (*They take*

their places.) That's right. Serve me last, Giulietta. Sandro is hungry.

SQUARCIO (*to the girl*): Come come! do you not see that his Excellency will touch nothing until we have had some first. (*He eats.*) See, Excellency! I have tasted everything. To tell you the truth, poisoning is an art I do not understand.

FERRUCCIO: Very few professional poisoners do, Squarcio. One of the best professionals in Rome poisoned my uncle and aunt. They are alive still. The poison cured my uncle's gout, and only made my aunt thin, which was exactly what she desired, poor lady, as she was losing her figure terribly.

SQUARCIO: There is nothing like the sword, Excellency.

SANDRO: Except the water, Father Squarcio. Trust a fisherman to know that. Nobody can tell that drowning was not an accident.

FERRUCCIO: What does Giulietta say?

GIULIA: I should not kill a man if I hated him. You cannot torment a man when he is dead. Men kill because they think it is what they call a satisfaction. But that is only fancy.

FERRUCCIO: And if you loved him? Would you kill him then?

GIULIA: Perhaps. If you love a man you are his slave: everything he says – everything he does – is a stab to your heart: every day is a long dread of losing him. Better kill him if there be no other escape.

FERRUCCIO: How well you have brought up your family, Squarcio! Some more omelet, Sandro?

SANDRO (*very cheerfully*): I thank your Excellency. (*He accepts and eats with an appetite.*)

FERRUCCIO: I pledge you all. To the sword and the fisherman's net: to love and hate! (*He drinks: they drink with him.*)

SQUARCIO: To the sword!

SANDRO: To the net, Excellency, with thanks for the honour.

GIULIA: To love, signor.

FERRUCCIO: To hate: the noble's portion!

SQUARCIO: The meal has done you good, Excellency. How do you feel now?

FERRUCCIO: I feel that there is nothing but a bait of ten crowns between me and death, Squarcio.

SQUARCIO: It is enough, Excellency. And enough is always enough.

SANDRO: Do not think of that, Excellency. It is only that we are poor folk, and have to consider how to make both ends meet as one may say. (*Looking at the dish.*) Excellency —?

FERRUCCIO: Finish it, Sandro. I've done.

SANDRO: Father Squarcio?

SQUARCIO: Finish it, finish it.

SANDRO: Giulietta?

GIULIA (*surprised*): Me? Oh no. Finish it, Sandro: it will only go to the pig.

SANDRO: Then, with your Excellency's permission — (*He helps himself.*)

SQUARCIO: Sing for his Excellency, my daughter.

GIULIA *turns to the door to fetch her mandoline.*

FERRUCCIO: I shall jump into the lake, Squarcio, if your cat begins to miaowl.

SANDRO (*always cheerful and reassuring*): No, no, Excellency: Giulietta sings very sweetly: have no fear.

FERRUCCIO: I do not care for singing: at least not the singing of peasants. There is only one thing for which one woman will do as well as another, and that is lovemaking. Come, Father Squarcio: I will buy Giulietta from you: you can have her back for nothing when I am tired of her. How much?

SQUARCIO: In ready money, or in promises?

FERRUCCIO: Old fox. Ready money.

SQUARCIO: Fifty crowns, Excellency.

FERRUCCIO: Fifty crowns! Fifty crowns for that blackfaced devil! I would not give fifty crowns for one of my mother's ladies-in-waiting. Fifty pence, you must mean.

SQUARCIO: Doubtless your Excellency, being a younger son, is poor. Shall we say five and twenty crowns?

FERRUCCIO: I tell you she is not worth five.

SQUARCIO: Oh, if you come to what she is worth, Excellency,

what are any of us worth? I take it that you are a gentleman, not
a merchant.

GIULIA: What are you worth, Signorino?

FERRUCCIO: I am accustomed to be asked for favours, Giuliaccia, not to be asked impertinent questions.

GIULIA: What would you do if a strong man took you by the
scruff of your neck, or his daughter thrust a knife in your
throat, Signor?

FERRUCCIO: It would be many a year, my gentle Giuliaccia,
before any baseborn man or woman would dare threaten a
nobleman again. The whole village would be flayed alive.

SANDRO: Oh no, Signor. These things often have a great air
of being accidents. And the great families are well content
that they should appear so. It is such a great trouble to flay
a whole village alive. Here by the water, accidents are so
common.

SQUARCIO: We of the nobility, Signor, are not strict enough. I
learnt that when I took to breeding horses. The horses you
breed from thoroughbreds are not all worth the trouble: most
of them are screws. Well, the horse-breeder gets rid of his
screws for what they will fetch: they go to labour like any
peasant's beast. But our nobility does not study its business so
carefully. If you are a screw, and the son of a baron, you are
brought up to think yourself a little god, though you are
nothing, and cannot rule yourself, much less a province. And
you presume, and presume, and presume —

GIULIA: And insult, and insult, and insult.

SQUARCIO: Until one day you find yourself in a strange place
with nothing to help you but your own hands and your own
wits —

GIULIA: And you perish —

SANDRO: Accidentally —

GIULIA: And your soul goes crying to your father for ven-
geance —

SQUARCIO: If indeed, my daughter, there be any soul left when
the body is slain.

FERRUCCIO (*crossing himself hastily*): Dog of a bandit: do you dare doubt the existence of God and the soul?

SQUARCIO: I think, Excellency, that the soul is so precious a gift that God will not give it to a man for nothing. He must earn it by being something and doing something. I should not like to kill a man with a good soul. I've had a dog that had, I'm persuaded, made itself something of a soul; and if anyone had murdered that dog, I would have slain him. But show me a man with no soul: one who has never done anything or been anything; and I will kill him for ten crowns with as little remorse as I would stick a pig.

SANDRO: Unless he be a nobleman, of course —

SQUARCIO: In which case the price is fifty crowns.

FERRUCCIO: Soul or no soul?

SQUARCIO: When it comes to a matter of fifty crowns, Excellency, business is business. The man who pays me must square the account with the devil. It is for my employer to consider whether the action be a good one or no: it is for me to earn his money honestly. When I said I should not like to kill a man with a good soul, I meant killing on my own account: not professionally.

FERRUCCIO: Are you such a fool then as to spoil your own trade by sometimes killing people for nothing?

SQUARCIO: One kills a snake for nothing, Excellency. One kills a dog for nothing sometimes.

SANDRO (*apologetically*): Only a mad dog, Excellency, of course.

SQUARCIO: A pet dog, too. One that eats and eats and is useless, and makes an honest man's house dirty. (*He rises.*) Come, Sandro, and help me to clean up. You, Giulia, stay and entertain his Excellency.

He and SANDRO *make a hammock of the cloth, in which they carry the wooden platters and fragments of the meal indoors.* FERRUCCIO *is left alone with* GIULIA. *The gloaming deepens.*

FERRUCCIO: Does you father do the housework with a great girl like you idling about? Squarcio is a fool, after all.

GIULIA: No, Signor: he has left me here to prevent you from escaping.

FERRUCCIO: There is nothing to be gained by killing me, Giuliaccia.

GIULIA: Perhaps; but I do not know. I saw Sandro make a sign to my father: that is why they went in. Sandro has something in his head.

FERRUCCIO (*brutally*): Lice, no doubt.

GIULIA (*unmoved*): That would only make him scratch his head, Signor, not make signs with it to my father. You did wrong to throw the Cardinal out of the window.

FERRUCCIO: Indeed: and pray why?

GIULIA: He will pay thirty crowns for your dead body. Then Sandro could marry me.

FERRUCCIO: And be broken on the wheel for it.

GIULIA: It would look like an accident, Signor. Sandro is very clever; and he is so humble and cheerful and good-tempered that people do not suspect him as they suspect my father.

FERRUCCIO: Giulietta: if I reach Sacromonte in safety, I swear to send you thirty crowns by a sure messenger within ten days. Then you can marry your Sandro. How does that appeal to you?

GIULIA: Your oath is not worth twenty pence, Signor.

FERRUCCIO: Do you think I will die here like a rat in a trap — (*His breath fails him.*)

GIULIA: Rats have to wait in their traps for death, Signor. Why not you?

FERRUCCIO: I'll fight.

GIULIA: You are welcome, Signor. The blood flows freest when it is hot.

FERRUCCIO: She devil! Listen to me, Giulietta —

GIULIA: It is useless, Signor. Giulietta or Giuliaccia: it makes no difference. If they two in there kill you it will be no more to me – except for the money – than if my father trod on a snail.

FERRUCCIO: Oh, it is not possible that I, a nobleman, should die by such filthy hands.

GIULIA: You have lived by them, Signor. I see no sign of any work on your own hands. We can bring death as well as life, we poor people, Signor.

FERRUCCIO: Mother of God, what shall I do?

GIULIA: Pray, Signor.

FERRUCCIO: Pray! With the taste of death in my mouth? I can think of nothing.

GIULIA: It is only that you have forgotten your beads, Signor. (*She picks up the Friar's rosary.*) You remember the old man's bones rattling. Here they are. (*She rattles them before him.*)

FERRUCCIO: That reminds me. I know of a painter in the north that can paint such beautiful saints that the heart goes out of one's body to look at them. If I get out of this alive I'll make him paint St Barbara so that everyone can see that she is lovelier than St Cecilia, who looks like my washerwoman's mother in her Chapel in our cathedral. Can you give St Cecilia a picture if she lets me be killed?

GIULIA: No; but I can give her many prayers.

FERRUCCIO: Prayers cost nothing. She will prefer the picture unless she is a greater fool than I take her to be.

GIULIA: She will thank the painter for it, not you, Signor. And I'll tell her in my prayers to appear to the painter in a vision, and order him to paint her just as he sees her if she really wishes to be painted.

FERRUCCIO: You are devilishly ready with your answers. Tell me, Giulietta: is what your father told me true? Is your blood really noble?

GIULIA: It is red, Signor, like the blood of the Christ in the picture in Church. I do not know if yours is different. I shall see when my father kills you.

FERRUCCIO: Do you know what I am thinking, Giulietta?

GIULIA: No, Signor.

FERRUCCIO: I am thinking that if the good God would oblige me by taking my fool of an elder brother up to heaven, and his silly doll of a wife with him before she has time to give him a son, you would make a rare duchess for me. Come! Will you help me to outwit your father and Sandro if I marry you afterwards?

GIULIA: No, Signor: I'll help them to kill you.

FERRUCCIO: My back is to the wall, then?

GIULIA: To the precipice, I think, Signor.

FERRUCCIO: No matter, so my face is to the danger. Did you notice, Giulia, a minute ago? I was frightened.

GIULIA: Yes, Signor. I saw it in your face.

FERRUCCIO: The terror of terrors.

GIULIA: The terror of death.

FERRUCCIO: No: death is nothing. I can face a stab just as I faced having my tooth pulled out at Faenza.

GIULIA (*shuddering with sincere sympathy*): Poor Signorino! That must have hurt horribly.

FERRUCCIO: What! You pity me for the tooth affair, and you did not pity me in that hideous agony of terror that is not the terror of death nor of anything else, but pure grim terror in itself.

GIULIA: It was the terror of the soul, Signor. And I do not pity your soul: you have a wicked soul. But you have pretty teeth.

FERRUCCIO: The toothache lasted a week; but the agony of my soul was too dreadful to last five minutes: I should have died of it if it could have kept its grip of me. But you helped me out of it.

GIULIA: I, Signor!

FERRUCCIO: Yes: you. If you had pitied me: if you had been less inexorable than death itself, I should have broken down and cried and begged for mercy. But now I have come up against something hard: something real: something that does not care for me. I see now the truth of my excellent uncle's opinion that I was a spoilt cub. When I wanted anything I threatened men or ran crying to women; and they gave it to me. I dreamed and romanced: imagining things as I wanted them, not as they

really are. There is nothing like a good look into the face of
death: close up: right on you: for showing you how little you
really believe and how little you really are. A priest said to me
once, 'In your last hour everything will fall away from you
except your religion.' But I have lived through my last hour;
and my religion was the first thing that fell away from me.
When I was forced at last to believe in grim death I knew at last
what belief was, and that I had never believed in anything
before: I had only flattered myself with pretty stories, and
sheltered myself behind Mumbo Jumbo, as a soldier will
shelter himself from arrows behind a clump of thistles that only
hide the shooters from him. When I believe in everything
that is real as I believed for that moment in death, then I
shall be a man at last. I have tasted the water of life from the cup
of death; and it may be now that my real life began with this
(*he holds up the rosary*) and will end with the triple crown or the
heretic's fire: I care not which. (*Springing to his feet.*) Come out,
then, dog of a bandit, and fight a man who has found his soul.
(SQUARCIO *appears at the door, sword in hand.* FERRUCCIO *leaps
at him and strikes him full in the chest with his dagger.* SQUARCIO
*puts back his left foot to brace himself against the shock. The dagger
snaps as if it had struck a stone wall.*)

GIULIA: Quick, Sandro.

SANDRO, *who has come stealing round the corner of the inn with a
fishing net, casts it over Ferruccio, and draws it tight.*

SQUARCIO: Your Excellency will excuse my shirt of mail. A
good home blow, nevertheless, Excellency.

SANDRO: Your Excellency will excuse my net: it is a little damp.

FERRUCCIO: Well, what now? Accidental drowning, I suppose.

SANDRO: Eh, Excellency, it is such a pity to throw a good fish
back into the water when once you have got him safe in your
net. My Giulietta: hold the net for me.

GIULIA (*taking the net and twisting it in her hands to draw it tighter
round him*): I have you very fast now, Signorino, like a little
bird in a cage.

FERRUCCIO: You have my body, Giulia. My soul is free.

GIULIA: Is it, Signor? I think Saint Barbara has got that in her net too. She has turned your jest into earnest.

SANDRO: It is indeed true, sir, that those who come under the special protection of God and the Saints are always a little mad; and this makes us think it very unlucky to kill a madman. And since from what Father Squarcio and I overheard, it is clear that your Excellency, though a very wise and reasonable young gentleman in a general way, is somewhat cracked on the subject of the soul and so forth, we have resolved to see that no harm comes to your Excellency.

FERRUCCIO: As you please. My life is only a drop falling from the vanishing clouds to the everlasting sea, from finite to infinite, and itself part of the infinite.

SANDRO (*impressed*): Your Excellency speaks like a crazy but very holy book. Heaven forbid that we should raise a hand against you! But your Excellency will notice that this good action will cost us thirty crowns.

FERRUCCIO: Is it not worth it?

SANDRO: Doubtless, doubtless. It will in fact save us the price of certain masses which we should otherwise have had said for the souls of certain persons who – ahem! Well, no matter. But we think it dangerous and unbecoming that a nobleman like your Excellency should travel without a retinue, and unarmed; for your dagger is unfortunately broken, Excellency. If you would therefore have the condescension to accept Father Squarcio as your man-at-arms – your servant in all but the name, to save his nobility – he will go with you to any town in which you will feel safe from His Eminence the Cardinal, and will leave it to your Excellency's graciousness as to whether his magnanimous conduct will not then deserve some trifling present: say a wedding gift for my Giulietta.

FERRUCCIO: Good: the man I tried to slay will save me from being slain. Who would have thought Saint Barbara so full of irony!

SANDRO: And if the offer your Excellency was good enough to make in respect of Giulietta still stands —

FERRUCCIO: Rascal: have you then no soul?

SANDRO: I am a poor man, Excellency: I cannot afford these luxuries of the rich.

FERRUCCIO: There is a certain painter will presently make a great picture of St Barbara; and Giulia will be his model. He will pay her well. Giulia: release the bird. It is time for it to fly. *She takes the net from his shoulders.*

The Dark Lady of the Sonnets

Trivial as this little play of mine is, its sketch of Shakespear is more complete than its levity suggests. . . . I had unfortunately represented Shakespear as treasuring and using (as I do myself) the jewels of unconsciously musical speech which common people utter and throw away every day; and this was taken as a disparagement of Shakespear's 'originality'. Why was I born with such contemporaries? Why is Shakespear made ridiculous by such a posterity?

CHARACTERS

WILLIAM SHAKESPEAR*
QUEEN ELIZABETH I
MARY FITTON
A BEEFEATER

SCENE: The terrace of Whitehall Palace. Midsummer night.

PERIOD: 1600.

Shaw wanted Ellen Terry to play the Queen in the original production at the Haymarket Theatre, London, 24 November 1910. In fact, the part was played by Suzanne Sheldon, with Granville-Barker in the part of Shakespear.

*Always spelt thus by Shaw.

THE DARK LADY OF THE SONNETS

The Dark Lady of the Sonnets must, surely, be Shaw's most famous one-act play; it is, in fact, one of the most famous one-act plays ever written.

In a long Preface to the play – a Preface twice as long as the play itself – Shaw tells us how the play originated. The idea of a contrived dramatic meeting between Shakespeare, Queen Elizabeth I and Mary Fitton (the legendary 'Dark Lady' of Shakespeare's sonnets) had been suggested to him by a friend. Shaw wrote the play as part of an entertainment intended to raise funds for a National Theatre project as a memorial to Shakespeare: a *pièce d'occasion* is what he so rightly calls it.

It was perfectly natural that Shaw should interest himself in such a project. As a youngster he spent many of his leisure hours in his native Dublin at the theatre: he particularly loved the plays of Shakespeare and knew many of them by heart. He certainly learnt a great deal from Shakespeare, particularly how to handle a dramatic situation. Like Shakespeare, too, he could fool and be serious in the same play without producing an incongruous effect. When he wrote *Caesar and Cleopatra*, an early play, he probably thought of himself as completing a trilogy, Shakespeare's *Julius Caesar* and *Antony and Cleopatra* being the other two parts. On two occasions he tackled blank verse in the manner of Shakespeare, and pretended that it was the easiest way of writing plays (adding with tongue in cheek that this explained Shakespeare's large output!): an early play, *The Admirable Bashville*, (1910), was hurriedly written in blank verse from an earlier novel he had written to prevent pirated dramatizations of it in the United States; later in life he entirely recast the Fifth Act of *Cymbeline* (1937) as he thought the original too full of improbabilities and complications. Obvious references in the text to the abdication crisis of the period prevented its being used as intended at Stratford; in a preface to the published version he makes it clear that he felt not a little ashamed of what he had done.

Perhaps Shaw had a nagging fear that posterity would deal harshly with him; that his reputation would suffer and decline over the years. At one time he linked his name with Aristophanes, Shakespeare and Moliere – and wondered if he would be remembered as long as they. Or would he be a 'forgotten clown' by the end of the century? I think Shaw's attitude to Shakespeare is best summed up in the lines he gives to Shav (himself) in a little puppet play, *Shakes v. Shav*, written by him towards the end of his life. Shakes has been railing against 'an infamous impostor . . . this fiend of Ireland'. Replies Shav:

> We are both mortal. For a moment suffer
> My glimmering light to shine.

THE DARK LADY OF THE SONNETS

Fin de siècle 15–1600. *Midsummer night on the terrace of the Palace at Whitehall, overlooking the Thames. The Palace clock chimes four quarters and strikes eleven.*

A BEEFEATER *on guard. A* CLOAKED MAN *approaches.*

THE BEEFEATER: Stand. Who goes there? Give the word.

THE MAN: Marry! I cannot. I have clean forgotten it.

THE BEEFEATER: Then you cannot pass here. What is your business? Who are you? Are you a true man?

THE MAN: Far from it, Master Warder. I am not the same man two days together: sometimes Adams, sometimes Benvolio, and anon the Ghost.

THE BEEFEATER (*recoiling*): A ghost! Angels and ministers of grace defend us!

THE MAN: Well said, Master Warder. With your leave I will set that down in writing; for I have a very poor and unhappy brain for remembrance. (*He takes out his tablets and writes.*) Methinks this is a good scene, with you on your lonely watch, and I approaching like a ghost in the moonlight. Stare not so amazedly at me; but mark what I say. I keep tryst here tonight with a dark lady. She promised to bribe the warder. I gave her the wherewithal: four tickets for the Globe Theatre.

THE BEEFEATER: Plague on her! She gave me two only.

THE MAN (*Detaching a tablet*): My friend: present this tablet, and you will be welcomed at any time when the plays of Will Shakespear are in hand. Bring your wife. Bring your friends. Bring the whole garrison. There is ever plenty of room.

THE BEEFEATER: I care not for these new-fangled plays. No

man can understand a word of them. They are all talk. Will you not give me a pass for The Spanish Tragedy?

THE MAN: To see The Spanish Tragedy one pays, my friend. Here are the means. (*He gives him a piece of gold.*)

THE BEEFEATER (*overwhelmed*): Gold! Oh, sir, you are a better paymaster than your dark lady.

THE MAN: Women are thrifty, my friend.

THE BEEFEATER: 'Tis so, sir. And you have to consider that the most open handed of us must een cheapen that which we buy every day. This lady has to make a present to a warder nigh every night of her life.

THE MAN (*turning pale*): I'll not believe it.

THE BEEFEATER: Now you, sir, I dare be sworn, do not have an adventure like this twice in the year.

THE MAN: Villain: wouldst tell me that my dark lady hath ever done thus before? that she maketh occasions to meet other men?

THE BEEFEATER: Now the Lord bless your innocence, sir, do you think you are the only pretty man in the world? A merry lady, sir: a warm bit of stuff. Go to: I'll not see her pass a deceit on a gentleman that hath given me the first piece of gold I ever handled.

THE MAN: Master Warder: is it not a strange thing that we, knowing that all women are false, should be amazed to find our own particular drab no better than the rest?

THE BEEFEATER: Not all, sir. Decent bodies, many of them.

THE MAN (*intolerantly*): No. All false. All. If thou deny it, thou liest.

THE BEEFEATER: You judge too much by the Court, sir. There indeed, you may say of frailty that its name is woman.

THE MAN (*pulling out his tablets again*): Prithee say that again: that about frailty: the strain of music.

THE BEEFEATER: What strain of music, sir? I'm no musician, God knows.

THE MAN: There is music in your soul: many of your degree have it very notably. (*Writing.*) 'Frailty: thy name is woman!' (*Repeating it affectionately.*) 'Thy name is woman.'

THE BEEFEATER: Well, sir, it is but four words. Are you a snapper-up of such unconsidered trifles?

THE MAN (*eagerly*): Snapper-up of — (*He gasps.*) Oh! Immortal phrase! (*He writes it down.*) This man is a greater than I.

THE BEEFEATER: You have my lord Pembroke's trick, sir.

THE MAN: Like enough: he is my near friend. But what call you his trick?

THE BEEFEATER: Making sonnets by moonlight. And to the same lady too.

THE MAN: No!

THE BEEFEATER: Last night he stood here on your errand, and in your shoes.

THE MAN: Thou, too, Brutus! And I called him friend!

THE BEEFEATER: 'Tis ever so, sir.

THE MAN: 'Tis ever so. 'Twas ever so. (*He turns away, overcome.*) Two Gentlemen of Verona! Judas! Judas!!

THE BEEFEATER: Is he so bad as that, sir?

THE MAN (*recovering his charity and self-possession*): Bad? O no. Human, Master Warder, human. We call one another names when we are offended, as children do. That is all.

THE BEEFEATER: Ay, sir: words, words, words. Mere wind, sir. We fill our bellies with the east wind, sir, as the Scripture hath it. You cannot feed capons so.

THE MAN: A good cadence. By your leave. (*He makes a note of it.*)

THE BEEFEATER: What manner of thing is a cadence, sir? I have not heard of it.

THE MAN: A thing to rule the world with, friend.

THE BEEFEATER: You speak strangely, sir: no offence. But, ain't like you, you are a very civil gentleman; and a poor man feels drawn to you, you being, as twere, willing to share your thought with him.

THE MAN: 'Tis my trade. But alas! the world for the most part will none of my thoughts.

Lamplight streams from the palace door as it opens from within.

THE BEEFEATER: Here comes your lady, sir. I'll do t'other end of my ward. You may een take your time about your business: I shall not return too suddenly unless my sergeant comes prowling round. 'Tis a fell sergeant, sir: strict in his arrest. Good een, sir; and good luck! (*He goes.*)

THE MAN: 'Strict in his arrest!' 'Fell sergeant!' (*As if tasting a ripe plum.*) O-o-o-h! (*He makes a note of them.*) *A* CLOAKED LADY *gropes her way from the palace and wanders along the terrace, walking in her sleep.*

THE LADY (*rubbing her hands as if washing them*): Out, damned spot. You will mar all with these cosmetics. God made you one face; and you make yourself another. Think of your grave, woman, not ever of being beautified. All the perfumes of Arabia will not whiten this Tudor hand.

THE MAN: 'All the perfumes of Arabia!' 'Beautified!' 'Beautified!' a poem in a single word. Can this by my Mary? (*To the Lady.*) Why do you speak in a strange voice, and utter poetry for the first time? Are you ailing? You walk like the dead. Mary! Mary!

THE LADY (*echoing him*): Mary! Mary! Who would have thought that woman to have had so much blood in her! Is it my fault that my counsellors put deeds of blood on me? Fie! If you were women you would have more wit than to stain the floor so foully. Hold not up her head so: the hair is false. I tell you yet again, Mary's buried: she cannot come out of her grave. I fear her not: these cats that dare jump into thrones though they be fit only for men's laps must be put away. What's done cannot be undone. Out, I say. Fie! a queen, and freckled!

THE MAN (*shaking her arm*): Mary, I say: art asleep?

THE LADY *wakes; starts; and nearly faints. He catches her on his arm.*

THE LADY: Where am I? What art thou?

THE MAN: I cry your mercy. I have mistook your person all this while. Methought you were my Mary: my mistress.

THE LADY (*outraged*): Profane fellow: how do you dare?

THE MAN: Be not wroth with me, lady. My mistress is a marvellous proper woman. But she does not speak so well as you.

'All the perfumes of Arabia!' That was well said: spoken with good accent and excellent discretion.

THE LADY: Have I been in speech with you here?

THE MAN: Why, yes, fair lady. Have you forgot it?

THE LADY: I have walked in my sleep.

THE MAN: Walk ever in your sleep, fair one; for then your words drop like honey.

THE LADY (*with cold majesty*): Know you to whom you speak, sir, that you dare express yourself so saucily?

THE MAN (*unabashed*): Not I, nor care neither. You are some lady of the Court, belike. To me there are but two sorts of women: those with excellent voices, sweet and low, and cackling hens that cannot make me dream. Your voice has all manner of loveliness in it. Grudge me not a short hour of its music.

THE LADY: Sir: you are overbold. Season your admiration for a while with —

THE MAN (*holding up his hand to stop her*): 'Season your admiration for a while —'

THE LADY: Fellow: do you dare mimic me to my face?

THE MAN: 'Tis music. Can you not hear? When a good musician sings a song, do you not sing it and sing it again 'til you have caught and fixed its perfect melody? 'Season your admiration for a while': God! the history of man's heart is in that one word admiration. Admiration! (*Taking up his tablets.*) What was it? 'Suspend your admiration for a space —'

THE LADY: A very vile jingle of esses. I said 'Season your —'

THE MAN (*hastily*) Season: ay, season, season, season. Plague on my memory, my wretched memory! I must een write it down. (*He begins to write, but stops, his memory failing him.*) Yet tell me which was the vile jingle? You said very justly: mine own ear caught it even as my false tongue said it.

THE LADY: You said 'for a space'. I said 'for a while'.

THE MAN: 'For a while' (*He corrects it.*) Good! (*Ardently.*) And now be mine neither for a space nor a while, but for ever.

THE LADY: Odds my life! Are you by chance making love to me, knave?

THE MAN: Nay: 'tis you who have made the love: I but pour it
out at your feet. I cannot but love a lass that sets such store by
an apt word. Therefore vouchsafe, divine perfection of a
woman – no: I have said that before somewhere; and the
wordy garment of my love for you must be fire-new —

THE LADY: You talk too much, sir. Let me warn you: I am
more accustomed to be listened to than preached at.

THE MAN: The most are like that that do talk well. But though
you spake with the tongues of angels, as indeed you do, yet
know that I am king of words —

THE LADY: A king, ha!

THE MAN: No less. We are poor things, we men and women —

THE LADY: Dare you call me woman?

THE MAN: What nobler name can I tender you? How else can I
love you? Yet you may well shrink from the name: have I not
said we are but poor things? Yet there is a power that can
redeem us.

THE LADY: Gramercy for your sermon, sir. I hope I know my
duty.

THE MAN: This is no sermon, but the living truth. The power
I speak of is the power of immortal poesy. For know that
vile as this world is, and worms as we are, you have but to
invest all this vileness with a magical garment of words to trans-
figure us and uplift our souls 'til earth flowers into a million
heavens.

THE LADY: You spoil your heaven with your million. You are
extravagant. Observe some measure in your speech.

THE MAN: You speak now as Ben does.

THE LADY: And who, pray, is Ben?

THE MAN: A learned bricklayer who thinks that the sky is at the
top of his ladder, and so takes it on him to rebuke me for
flying. I tell you there is no word yet coined and no melody yet
sung that is extravagant and majestical enough for the glory
that lovely words can reveal. It is heresy to deny it: have you
not been taught that in the beginning was the Word? that the
Word was with God? nay, that the Word was God?

THE LADY: Beware, fellow, how you presume to speak of holy things. The Queen is the head of the Church.

THE MAN: You are the head of my Church when you speak as you did at first. 'All the perfumes of Arabia!' Can the Queen speak thus? They say she playeth well upon the virginals. Let her play so to me; and I'll kiss her hands. But until then, you are my Queen; and I'll kiss those lips that have dropt music on my heart. (*He puts his arms about her.*)

THE LADY: Unmeasured impudence! On your life, take your hands from me.

The DARK LADY *comes stooping along the terrace behind them like a running thrush. When she sees how they are employed, she rises angrily to her full height, and listens jealously.*

THE MAN (*unaware of the Dark Lady*): Then cease to make my hands tremble with the streams of life you poured through them. You hold me as the lodestar holds the iron: I cannot but cling to you. We are lost, you and I: nothing can separate us now.

THE DARK LADY: We shall see that, false lying hound, you and your filthy trull. (*With two vigorous cuffs, she knocks the pair asunder, sending the man, who is unlucky enough to receive a right-handed blow, sprawling on the flags.*) Take that, both of you!

THE CLOAKED LADY (*in towering wrath, throwing off her cloak and turning in outraged majesty on her assailant*): High treason!

THE DARK LADY (*recognizing her and falling on her knees in abject terror*): Will: I am lost: I have struck the Queen.

THE MAN (*sitting up as majestically as his ignominious posture allows*): Woman: you have struck WILLIAM SHAKESPEAR!!!!!!

QUEEN ELIZABETH (*stupent*): Marry, come up!!! Struck William Shakespear quotha! And who in the name of all the sluts and jades and light-o'-loves and fly-by-nights that infest this palace of mine, may William Shakespear be?

THE DARK LADY: Madam: he is but a player. Oh, I could have my hand cut off —

QUEEN ELIZABETH: Belike you will, Mistress. Have you

bethought you that I am like to have your head cut off as well?

THE DARK LADY: Will: save me. Oh, save me.

ELIZABETH: Save you! A likely saviour, on my royal word! I had thought this fellow at least an esquire; for I had hoped that even the vilest of my ladies would not have dishonoured my Court by wantoning with a baseborn servant.

SHAKESPEAR (*indignantly scrambling to his feet*): Baseborn! I, a Shakespear of Stratford! I, whose mother was an Arden! baseborn! You forget yourself, Madam.

ELIZABETH (*furious*): S'blood! do I so? I will teach you —

THE DARK LADY (*rising from her knees and throwing herself between them*): Will: in God's name anger her no further. It is death. Madam: do not listen to him.

SHAKESPEAR: Not were it een to save your life, Mary, not to mention mine own, will I flatter a monarch who forgets what is due to my family. I deny not that my father was brought down to be a poor bankrupt; but 'twas his gentle blood that was ever too generous for trade. Never did he disown his debts. 'Tis true he paid them not; but it is an attested truth that he gave bills for them; and 'twas those bills, in the hands of base hucksters, that were his undoing.

ELIZABETH (*grimly*): The son of your father shall learn his place in the presence of the daughter of Harry the Eighth.

SHAKESPEAR (*swelling with intolerant importance*): Name not that inordinate man in the same breath with Stratford's worthiest alderman. John Shakespear wedded but once: Harry Tudor was married six times. You should blush to utter his name.

THE DARK LADY ⎱ *crying out*   Will: for pity's sake —
ELIZABETH   ⎰   *together*   Insolent dog —

SHAKESPEAR (*cutting them short*): How know you that King Harry was indeed your father?

ELIZABETH   ⎤ Zounds! Now by — (*She stops to grind her
                          ⎬ teeth with rage.*)
THE DARK LADY ⎦ She will have me whipped through the
                            streets. Oh God! Oh God!

SHAKESPEAR: Learn to know yourself better, Madam. I am an honest gentleman of unquestioned parentage, and have already sent in my demand for the coat-of-arms that is lawfully mine. Can you say as much for yourself?

ELIZABETH (*almost beside herself*): Another word; and I begin with mine own hands the work the hangman shall finish.

SHAKESPEAR: You are no true Tudor: this baggage here has as good a right to your royal seat as you. What maintains you on the throne of England? Is it your renownéd wit? your wisdom that sets at nought the craftiest statesmen of the Christian world? No. 'Tis the mere chance that might have happened to any milkmaid, the caprice of Nature that made you the most wondrous piece of beauty the age hath seen. (ELIZABETH'S *raised fists, on the point of striking him, fall to her side.*) That is what hath brought all men to your feet, and founded your throne on the impregnable rock of your proud heart, a stony island in a sea of desire. There, Madam, is some wholesome blunt honest speaking for you. Now do your worst.

ELIZABETH (*with dignity*): Master Shakespear: it is well for you that I am a merciful prince. I make allowance for your rustic ignorance. But remember that there are things which be true, and are yet not seemly to be said (I will not say to a queen; for you will have it that I am none) but to a virgin.

SHAKESPEAR (*bluntly*): It is no fault of mine that you are a virgin, Madam, albeit 'tis my misfortune.

THE DARK LADY (*terrified again*): In mercy, Madam, hold no further discourse with him. He hath ever some lewd jest on his tongue. You hear how he useth me! calling me baggage and like to your Majesty's face.

ELIZABETH: As for you, Mistress, I have yet to demand what your business is at this hour in this place, and how you come to be so concerned with a player that you strike blindly at your sovereign in your jealousy of him.

THE DARK LADY: Madam: as I live and hope for salvation —

SHAKESPEAR (*sardonically*): Ha!

THE DARK LADY (*angrily*): – ay, I'm as like to be saved as thou that believest naught save some black magic of words and verses – I say, Madam, as I am a living woman I came here to break with him for ever. Oh, Madam, if you would know what misery is, listen to this man that is more than man and less at the same time. He will tie you down to anatomize your very soul: he will wring tears of blood from your humiliation; and then he will heal the wound with flatteries that no woman can resist.

SHAKESPEAR: Flatteries! (*Kneeling.*) Oh, Madam, I put my case at your royal feet. I confess to much. I have a rude tongue: I am unmannerly: I blaspheme against the holiness of anointed royalty; but oh, my royal mistress, AM I a flatterer?

ELIZABETH: I absolve you as to that. You are far too plain a dealer to please me. (*He rises gratefully.*)

THE DARK LADY: Madam: he is flattering you even as he speaks.

ELIZABETH (*a terrible flash in her eye*): Ha! Is it so?

SHAKESPEAR: Madam: she is jealous; and, heaven help me! not without reason. Oh, you say you are a merciful prince; but that was cruel of you, that hiding of your royal dignity when you found me here. For how can I ever be content with this black-haired, black-eyed, black-avised devil again now that I have looked upon real beauty and real majesty?

THE DARK LADY (*wounded and desperate*): He hath swore to me ten times over that the day shall come in England when black women, for all their foulness, shall be more thought on than fair ones. (*To Shakespear, scolding at him.*) Deny it if thou canst. Oh, he is compact of lies and scorns. I am tired of being tossed up to heaven and dragged down to hell at every whim that takes him. I am ashamed to my very soul that I have abased myself to love one that my father would not have deemed fit to hold my stirrup – one that will talk to all the world about me – that will put my love and my shame into his plays and make me blush for myself there – that will write sonnets about me that no man of gentle strain would put his hand to. I am all disordered: I know not what I am saying to your Majesty: I am of all ladies most deject and wretched —

SHAKESPEAR: Ha! At last sorrow hath struck a note of music out of thee. 'Of all ladies most deject and wretched.' (*He makes a note of it.*)

THE DARK LADY: Madam: I implore you give me leave to go. I am distracted with grief and shame. I —

ELIZABETH: Go. (*The* DARK LADY *tries to kiss her hand.*) No more. Go. (*The* DARK LADY *goes, convulsed.*) You have been cruel to that poor fond wretch, Master Shakespear.

SHAKESPEAR: I am not cruel, Madam; but you know the fable of Jupiter and Semele. I could not help my lightnings scorching her.

ELIZABETH: You have an overweening conceit of yourself, sir, that displeases your Queen.

SHAKESPEAR: Oh, Madam, can I go about with the modest cough of a minor poet, belittling my inspiration and making the mightiest wonder of your reign a thing of nought? I have said that 'not marble nor the gilded monuments of princes shall out-live' the words with which I make the world glorious or foolish at my will. Besides, I would have you think me great enough to grant me a boon.

ELIZABETH: I hope it is a boon that may be asked of a virgin Queen without offence, sir. I mistrust your forwardness; and I bid you remember that I do not suffer persons of your degree (if I may say so without offence to your father the alderman) to presume too far.

SHAKESPEAR: Oh, Madam, I shall not forget myself again; though by my life, could I make you a serving wench, neither a queen nor a virgin should you be for so much longer as a flash of lightning might take to cross the river to the Bankside. But since you are a queen and will none of me, nor of Philip of Spain, nor of any other mortal man, I must een contain myself as best I may, and ask you only for a boon of State.

ELIZABETH: A boon of State already! You are becoming a courtier like the rest of them. You lack advancement.

SHAKESPEAR: 'Lack advancement.' By your Majesty's leave: a queenly phrase. (*He is about to write it down.*)

ELIZABETH (*striking the tablets from his hand*): Your tables begin to anger me, sir. I am not here to write your plays for you.

SHAKESPEAR: You are here to inspire them, Madam. For this, among the rest, were you ordained. But the boon I crave is that you do endow a great playhouse, or, if I may make bold to coin a scholarly name for it, a National Theatre, for the better instruction and gracing of your Majesty's subjects.

ELIZABETH: Why, sir, are there not theatres enow on the Bankside and in Blackfriars?

SHAKESPEAR: Madam: these are the adventures of needy and desperate men that must, to save themselves from perishing of want, give the sillier sort of people what they best like; and what they best like, God knows, is not their own betterment and instruction, as we well see by the example of the churches, which must needs compel men to frequent them, though they be open to all without charge. Only when there is a matter of a murder, or a plot, or a pretty youth in petticoats, or some naughty tale of wantonness, will your subjects pay the great cost of good players and their finery, with a little profit to boot. To prove this I will tell you that I have written two noble and excellent plays setting forth the advancement of women of high nature and fruitful industry even as your Majesty is: the one skilful physician, the other a sister devoted to good works. I have also stole from a book of idle wanton tales two of the most damnable foolishnesses in the world, in the one of which a woman goeth in man's attire and maketh impudent love to her swain, who pleaseth the groundlings by overthrowing a wrestler: whilst, in the other, one of the same kidney showeth her wit by saying endless naughtinesses to a gentleman as lewd as herself. I have writ these to save my friends from penury, yet shewing my scorn for such follies and for them that praise them by calling the one As You Like It, meaning that it is not as *I* like it, and the other Much Ado About Nothing, as it truly is. And now these two filthy pieces drive their nobler fellows from the stage, where indeed I cannot have my lady physician presented at all, she being too honest a woman for the taste of the town. Wherefore I humbly beg your Majesty to give order that a theatre be endowed out of the public revenue for the playing of those pieces of mine which no merchant will touch, seeing that his gain is so much greater with the worse than with the better. Thereby you shall also encourage other men to undertake the writing of plays who do now despise it and leave it wholly to those whose counsels will work little good to your realm. For this writing of plays is a great matter, forming as it does the minds and affections of men in such sort that whatsoever they see done in show on the stage, they will presently be doing in earnest in the world, which is but a larger stage. Of late, as you know, the Church taught the people by means of plays; but the people flocked only to such as were full of superstitious miracles and bloody martyrdoms; and so the Church, which also was just then brought into straits by the policy of your royal father, did abandon and discountenance the art of playing; and thus it fell into the hands of poor players and greedy merchants that had their pockets to look to and not the greatness of this your kingdom. Therefore now must your Majesty take up that good work that your Church hath abandoned, and restore the art of playing to its former use and dignity.

ELIZABETH: Master Shakespear: I will speak of this matter to the Lord Treasurer.

SHAKESPEAR: Then am I undone, Madam; for there was never yet a Lord Treasurer that could find a penny for anything over and above the necessary expenses of your government, save for a war or a salary for his own nephew.

ELIZABETH: Master Shakespear: you speak sooth; yet cannot I in any wise mend it. I dare not offend my unruly Puritans by making so lewd a place as the playhouse a public charge; and there be a thousand things to be done in this London of mine before your poetry can have its penny from the general purse. I tell thee, Master Will, it will be three hundred years and more before my subjects learn that man cannot live by bread alone, but by every word that cometh from the mouth of those whom

God inspires. By that time you and I will be dust beneath the feet of the horses, if indeed there be any horses then, and men be still riding instead of flying. Now it may be that by then your works will be dust also.

SHAKESPEAR: They will stand, Madam: fear not for that.

ELIZABETH: It may prove so. But of this I am certain (for I know my countrymen) that until every other country in the Christian world, even to barbarian Muscovy and the hamlets of the boorish Germans, have its playhouse at the public charge, England will never adventure. And she will adventure then only because it is her desire to be ever in the fashion, and do humbly and dutifully whatso she seeth everybody else doing. In the meantime you must content yourself as best you can by the playing of those two pieces which you give out as the most damnable ever writ, but which your countrymen, I warn you, will swear are the best you have ever done. But this I will say, that if I could speak across the ages to our descendants, I should heartily recommend them to fulfil your wish; for the Scottish minstrel hath well said that he that maketh the songs of a nation is mightier than he that maketh its laws; and the same may well be true of plays and interludes. (*The clock chimes the first quarter. The warder returns on his round.*) And now, sir, we are upon the hour when it better beseems a virgin queen to be abed than to converse alone with the naughtiest of her subjects. Ho there! Who keeps ward on the queen's lodgings tonight?

THE WARDER: I do, an't please your majesty.

ELIZABETH: See that you keep it better in future. You have let pass a most dangerous gallant even to the very door of our royal chamber. Lead him forth; and bring me word when he is safely locked out; for I shall scarce dare disrobe until the palace gates are between us.

SHAKESPEAR (*kissing her hand*): My body goes through the gate into the darkness, Madam; but my thoughts follow you.

ELIZABETH: How! to my bed!

SHAKESPEAR: No, Madam, to your prayers, in which I beg you to remember my theatre.

ELIZABETH: That is my prayer to posterity. Forget not your own to God; and so goodnight, Master Will.

SHAKESPEAR: Goodnight, great Elizabeth. God save the Queen!

ELIZABETH. Amen.

Exeunt severally: she to her chamber: he, in custody of the warder, to the gate nearest Blackfriars.

Augustus Does His Bit

A True-to-life Farce

The showing-up of Augustus scandalized one or two
innocent and patriotic critics who regarded the prowess of
the British Army as inextricably bound up with Highcastle
prestige. But our Government departments knew better:
their problem was how to win the war with Augustus on
their backs.

CHARACTERS

LORD AUGUSTUS HIGHCASTLE
HORATIO FLOYD BEAMISH, *a Clerk*
THE LADY

SCENE: The Mayor's parlour, the Town Hall, Little Pifflington.

TIME: 1916.

The play was first performed at the Court Theatre, London, by the Stage Society on 21 January 1917.

AUGUSTUS DOES HIS BIT

Government officials have always been fair game for the dramatist, especially where they combine with their officialdom such shortcomings as pomposity and officiousness. This has been so throughout the ages. Shaw is here poking fun (as only an Irishman can) at the English governing class, 'well-meaning, brave, patriotic, but obstructively fussy, self-important, imbecile and disastrous'. In 1917 he saw that such officials were a positive hindrance to the war effort.

Shaw's attack is never malicious: he is quite happy to expose the follies of the system as he sees it by laughing at it, and by getting us to laugh at it with him. He often did this. He himself had had experience of petty officialdom in 1917 when he visited the front-line in Flanders, having had first to spend several days in a tangle of red-tape, obtaining passes, permits, and suchlike.

This play is little more than a sketch; it is a farce and must be played as such. It will stand or fall according to the performance of the lady who must radiate 'personality'; success depends on her. Otherwise there should be no problems of production. The set must be realistic but no particular difficulties should arise; with limited facilities it can be modified but must present a Town Hall-cum-Government office atmosphere.

If Shaw seriously intended that the play would do any more than amuse, then he was sorely disappointed: 'Save for the satisfaction of being able to laugh at Augustus in the theatre, nothing, as far as I know, came of my dramatic reduction of him to absurdity . . . Augustus stood like the Eddystone in a storm, and stands so to this day. He gave us his word that he was indispensable; and we took it.'

AUGUSTUS DOES HIS BIT

The Mayor's parlour in the Town Hall of Little Pifflington. LORD
AUGUSTUS HIGHCASTLE, *a distinguished member of the governing
class, in the uniform of a colonel, and very well preserved at forty-five, is
comfortably seated at a writing table with his heels on it, reading* The
Morning Post. *The door faces him, a little to his left, at the other side
of the room. The window is behind him. In the fireplace, a gas stove. On
the table a bell button and a telephone. Portraits of past Mayors, in
robes and gold chains, adorn the walls. An elderly clerk with a short
white beard and whiskers, and a very red nose, shuffles in.*

AUGUSTUS (*hastily putting aside his paper and replacing his feet on the
floor*): Hullo! Who are you?

THE CLERK: The staff (*A slight impediment in his speech adds to the
impression of incompetence produced by his age and appearance.*)

AUGUSTUS: You the staff! What do you mean, man?

THE CLERK: What I say. There ain't anybody else.

AUGUSTUS: Tush! Where are the others?

THE CLERK: At the front.

AUGUSTUS: Quite right. Most proper. Why arn't you at the
front?

THE CLERK: Over age. Fifty-seven.

AUGUSTUS: But you can still do your bit. Many an older man is
in the G.R.'s, or volunteering for home defence.

THE CLERK: I have volunteered.

AUGUSTUS: Then why are you not in uniform?

THE CLERK: They said they wouldn't have me if I was given
away with a pound of tea. Told me to go home and not be an
old silly. (*A sense of unbearable wrong, till now only smouldering in
him, bursts into flame.*) Young Bill Knight, that I took with me,

got two and sevenpence. I got nothing. Is it justice? This country is going to the dogs, if you ask me.

AUGUSTUS (*rising indignantly*): I do not ask you, sir; I will not allow you to say such things in my presence. Our statesmen are the greatest known to history. Our generals are invincible. Our army is the admiration of the world. (*Furiously.*) How dare you tell me that the country is going to the dogs!

THE CLERK: Why did they give young Bill Knight two and sevenpence, and not give me even my tram fare? Do you call that being great statesmen? As good as robbing me, I call it.

AUGUSTUS: That's enough, Leave the room. (*He sits down and takes up his pen, settling himself to work.* THE CLERK *shuffles to the door.* AUGUSTUS *adds, with cold politeness*): Send me the Secretary.

THE CLERK: I'm the Secretary. I can't leave the room and send myself to you at the same time, can I?

AUGUSTUS: Don't be insolent. Where is the gentleman I have been corresponding with: Mr Horatio Floyd Beamish?

THE CLERK (*returning and bowing*): Here. Me.

AUGUSTUS: You! Ridiculous. What right have you to call yourself by a pretentious name of that sort?

THE CLERK: You may drop the Horatio Floyd. Beamish is good enough for me.

AUGUSTUS: Is there nobody else to take my instructions?

THE CLERK: It's me or nobody. And for two pins I'd chuck it. Don't you drive me too far. Old uns like me is up in the world now.

AUGUSTUS: If we were not at war. I should discharge you on the spot for disrespectful behaviour. But England is in danger; and I cannot think of my personal dignity at such a moment. (*Shouting at him.*) Don't you think of yours, either, worm that you are; or I'll have you arrested under the Defence of the Realm Act, double quick.

THE CLERK: What do I care about the realm? They done me out of two and seven —

AUGUSTUS: Oh, damn your two and seven! Did you receive my letters?

THE CLERK: Yes.

AUGUSTUS: I addressed a meeting here last night – went straight to the platform from the train. I wrote to you that I should expect you to be present and report yourself. Why did you not do so?

THE CLERK: The police wouldn't let me on the platform.

AUGUSTUS: Did you tell them who you were?

THE CLERK: They knew who I was. That's why they wouldn't let me up.

AUGUSTUS: This is too silly for anything. This town wants waking up. I made the best recruiting speech I ever made in my life; and not a man joined.

THE CLERK: What did you expect? You told them our gallant fellows is falling at the rate of a thousand a day in the big push. Dying for Little Pifflington, you says. Come and take their places, you says. That ain't the way to recruit.

AUGUSTUS: But I expressly told them their widows would have pensions.

THE CLERK: I heard you. Would have been all right if it had been the widows you wanted to get round.

AUGUSTUS (rising angrily): This town is inhabited by dastards. I say it with a full sense of responsibility, dastards! They call themselves Englishmen; and they are afraid to fight.

THE CLERK: Afraid to fight! You should see them on a Saturday night.

AUGUSTUS: Yes: they fight one another; but they won't fight the Germans.

THE CLERK: They got grudges again one another: how can they have grudges again the Huns that they never saw? They've no imagination: that's what it is. Bring the Huns here; and they'll quarrel with them fast enough.

AUGUSTUS (returning to his seat with a grunt of disgust): Mf! They'll have them here if they're not careful. (Seated.) Have you carried out my orders about the war saving.

THE CLERK: Yes.

AUGUSTUS: The allowance of petrol has been reduced by three-quarters?

THE CLERK: It has.

AUGUSTUS: And you have told the motor-car people to come here and arrange to start munition work now that their motor business is stopped?

THE CLERK: It ain't stopped. They're busier than ever.

AUGUSTUS: Busy at what?

THE CLERK: Making small cars.

AUGUSTUS: New cars!

THE CLERK: The old cars only do twelve miles to the gallon. Everybody has to have a car that will do thirty-five now.

AUGUSTUS: Can't they take the train?

THE CLERK: There ain't no trains now. They've tore up the rails and sent them to the front.

AUGUSTUS: Psha!

THE CLERK: Well, we have to get about somehow.

AUGUSTUS: This is perfectly monstrous. Not in the least what I intended.

THE CLERK: Hell —

AUGUSTUS: Sir!

THE CLERK (*explaining*): Hell, they says, is paved with good intentions.

AUGUSTUS (*springing to his feet*): Do you mean to insinuate that hell is paved with my good intentions – with the good intentions of His Majesty's Government?

THE CLERK: I don't mean to insinuate anything until the Defence of the Realm Act is repealed. It ain't safe.

AUGUSTUS: They told me that this town had set an example to all England in the matter of economy. I came down here to promise the Mayor a knighthood for his exertions.

THE CLERK: The Mayor! Where do I come in?

AUGUSTUS: You don't come in. You go out. This is a fool of a place. I'm greatly disappointed. Deeply disappointed. (*Flinging himself back into his chair.*) Disgusted.

THE CLERK: What more can we do? We've shut up everything. The picture gallery is shut. The museum is shut. The theatres and picture shows is shut: I haven't seen a movy picture for six months.

AUGUSTUS: Man, man: do you want to see picture shows when the Hun is at the gate?

THE CLERK (*mournfully*): I don't now, though it drove me melancholy mad at first. I was on the point of taking a pennorth of rat poison —

AUGUSTUS: Why didn't you?

THE CLERK: Because a friend advised me to take to drink instead. That saved my life, though it makes me very poor company in the mornings, as (*Hiccuping.*) perhaps you've noticed.

AUGUSTUS: Well, upon my soul! You are not ashamed to stand there and confess yourself a disgusting drunkard.

THE CLERK: Well, what of it? We're at war now; and everything's changed. Besides, I should lose my job here if I stood drinking at the bar. I'm a respectable man and must buy my drink and take it home with me. And they won't serve me with less than a quart. If you'd told me before the war that I could get through a quart of whisky in a day, I shouldn't have believed you. That's the good of war: it brings out powers in a man that he never suspected himself capable of. You said so yourself in your speech last night.

AUGUSTUS: I did not know that I was talking to an imbecile. You ought to be ashamed of yourself. There must be an end of this drunken slacking. I'm going to establish a new order of things here. I shall come down every morning before breakfast until things are properly in train. Have a cup of coffee and two rolls for me here every morning at half past ten.

THE CLERK: You can't have no rolls. The only baker that baked rolls was a Hun; and he's been interned.

AUGUSTUS: Quite right, too. And was there no Englishman to take his place?

THE CLERK: There was. But he was caught spying; and they took him up to London and shot him.

AUGUSTUS: Shot an Englishman!

THE CLERK: Well, it stands to reason if the Germans wanted a spy they wouldn't employ a German that everybody would suspect, don't it?

AUGUSTUS (*rising again*): Do you mean to say, you scoundrel, that an Englishman is capable of selling his country to the enemy for gold?

THE CLERK: Not as a general thing I wouldn't say it; but there's men here would sell their own mothers for two coppers if they got the chance.

AUGUSTUS: Beamish: it's an ill bird that fouls its own nest.

THE CLERK: It wasn't me that let Little Pifflington get foul. *I* don't belong to the governing classes. I only tell you why you can't have no rolls.

AUGUSTUS (*intensely irritated*): Can you tell me where I can find an intelligent being to take my orders?

THE CLERK: One of the street sweepers used to teach in the school until it was shut up for the sake of economy. Will he do?

AUGUSTUS: What! You mean to tell me that when the lives of the gallant fellows in our trenches, and the fate of the British Empire, depend on our keeping up the supply of shells, you are wasting money on sweeping the streets?

THE CLERK: We have to. We dropped it for a while; but the infant death rate went up something frightful.

AUGUSTUS: What matters the death rate of Little Pifflington in a moment like this? Think of our gallant soldiers, not of your squalling infants.

THE CLERK: If you want soldiers you must have children. You can't buy 'em in boxes, like toy soldiers.

AUGUSTUS: Beamish: the long and the short of it is, you are no patriot. Go downstairs to your office; and have that gas stove taken away and replaced by an ordinary grate. The Board of Trade has urged on me the necessity for economizing gas.

THE CLERK: Our orders from the Minister of Munitions is to use gas instead of coal, because it saves material. Which is it to be?

AUGUSTUS (*bawling furiously at him*): Both! Don't criticize your orders: obey them. Yours not to reason why: yours but to do and die. That's war. (*Cooling down.*) Have you anything else to say?

THE CLERK: Yes: I want a rise.

AUGUSTUS (*reeling against the table in his horror*): A rise! Horatio Floyd Beamish: do you know that we are at war?

THE CLERK (*feebly ironical*): I have noticed something about it in the papers. Heard you mention it once or twice, now I come to think of it.

AUGUSTUS: Our gallant fellows are dying in the trenches; and you want a rise!

THE CLERK: What are they dying for? To keep me alive, ain't it? Well, what's the good of that if I'm dead of hunger by the time they come back?

AUGUSTUS: Everybody else is making sacrifices without a thought of self; and you —

THE CLERK: Not half, they ain't. Where's the baker's sacrifice? Where's the coal merchant's? Where's the butcher's? Charging me double: that's how they sacrifice themselves. Well, I want to sacrifice myself that way too. Just double next Saturday: double and not a penny less; or no secretary for you. (*He stiffens himself shakily, and makes resolutely for the door.*)

AUGUSTUS (*looking after him contemptuously*): Go: miserable pro-German.

THE CLERK (*rushing back and facing him*): Who are you calling a pro-German?

AUGUSTUS: Another word, and I charge you under the Act with discouraging me. Go.

THE CLERK *blenches and goes out, cowed.*

The telephone rings.

AUGUSTUS (*taking up the telephone receiver*): Hallo ... Yes: who are you? ... oh, Blueloo, is it? ... Yes: there's nobody in the room: fire away ... What? ... A spy! ... A woman! ... Yes: I brought it down with me. Do you suppose I'm such a fool as to let it out of my hands? Why, it gives a list of all our anti-aircraft emplacements from Ramsgate to Skegness. The Germans would give a million for it – what? . . . But how could she possibly know about it? I haven't mentioned it to a soul, except, of course, dear Lucy. . . . Oh, Toto and Lady Popham and that lot: they don't count: they're all right. I mean that I haven't mentioned it to any Germans. . . . Pooh! Don't you be nervous, old chap. I know you think me a fool: but I'm not such a fool as all that. If she tries to get it out of me I'll have her in the Tower before you ring up again. (THE CLERK *returns.*) Sh-sh! Somebody's just come in: ring off. Goodbye. (*He hangs up the receiver.*)

THE CLERK: Are you engaged? (*His manner is strangely softened.*)

AUGUSTUS: What business is that of yours? However, if you will take the trouble to read the society papers for this week, you will see that I am engaged to the Honourable Lucy Popham, youngest daughter of —

THE CLERK: That ain't what I mean. Can you see a female?

AUGUSTUS: Of course I can see a female as easily as a male. Do you suppose I'm blind?

THE CLERK: You don't seem to follow me, somehow. There's a female downstairs: what you might call a lady. She wants to know can you see her if I let her up.

AUGUSTUS: Oh, you mean am I disengaged. Tell the lady I have just received news of the greatest importance which will occupy my entire attention for the rest of the day, and that she must write for an appointment.

THE CLERK: I'll ask her to explain her business to me. *I* ain't above talking to a handsome young female when I get the chance. (*Going.*)

AUGUSTUS: Stop. Does she seem to be a person of consequence?

THE CLERK: A regular marchioness, if you ask me.

AUGUSTUS: Hm! Beautiful, did you say?

THE CLERK: A human chrysanthemum, sir, believe me.

AUGUSTUS: It will be extremely inconvenient for me to see her; but the country is in danger; and we must not consider our own comfort. Think how our gallant fellows are suffering in the trenches! Show her up. (THE CLERK *makes for the door, whistling the latest popular love ballad.*) Stop whistling instantly, sir. This is not a casino.

THE CLERK: Ain't it? You just wait 'til you see her. (*He goes out.*) AUGUSTUS *produces a mirror, a comb, and a pot of moustache pomade from the drawer of the writing-table, and sits down before the mirror to put some touches to his toilet.*

THE CLERK *returns, devotedly ushering a very attractive lady, brilliantly dressed. She has a dainty wallet hanging from her wrist.* AUGUSTUS *hastily covers up his toilet apparatus with* The Morning Post, *and rises in an attitude of pompous condescension.*

THE CLERK (*to Augustus*): Here she is. (*To the lady.*) May I offer you a chair, lady? (*He places a chair at the writing-table opposite Augustus, and steals out on tiptoe.*)

AUGUSTUS: Be seated, Madam.

THE LADY (*sitting down*): Are you Lord Augustus Highcastle?

AUGUSTUS (*sitting also*): Madam: I am.

THE LADY (*with awe*): The great Lord Augustus?

AUGUSTUS: I should not dream of describing myself so, Madam; but no doubt I have impressed my countrymen – and (*Bowing gallantly.*) may I say my countrywomen – as having some exceptional claims to their consideration.

THE LADY (*emotionally*): What a beautiful voice you have!

AUGUSTUS: What you hear, Madam, is the voice of my country, which now takes a sweet and noble tone even in the harsh mouth of high officialism.

THE LADY: Please go on. You express yourself so wonderfully.

AUGUSTUS: It would be strange indeed if, after sitting on thirty-seven Royal Commissions, mostly as chairman, I had not mastered the art of public expression. Even the Radical papers have paid me the high compliment of declaring that I am never more impressive than when I have nothing to say.

THE LADY: I never read the Radical papers. All I can tell you is that what we women admire in you is not the politician, but the man of action, the heroic warrior, the *beau sabreur*.

AUGUSTUS (*gloomily*): Madam, I beg! Please! My military exploits are not a pleasant subject, unhappily.

THE LADY: Oh, I know, I know. How shamefully you have been treated! What ingratitude! But the country is with you. The women are with you. Oh, do you think all our hearts did not throb and all our nerves thrill when we heard how, when you were ordered to occupy that terrible quarry in Hulluch, and you swept into it at the head of your men like a sea-god riding on a tidal wave, you suddenly sprang over the top shouting 'To Berlin! Forward!'; dashed at the German army single-handed; and were cut off and made prisoner by the Huns?

AUGUSTUS: Yes, Madam; and what was my reward? They said I had disobeyed orders, and sent me home. Have they forgotten Nelson in the Baltic? Has any British battle ever been won except by a bold individual initiative? I say nothing of professional jealousy: it exists in the army as elsewhere; but it is a bitter thought to me that the recognition denied me by my own country – or rather by the Radical cabal in the Cabinet which pursues my family with rancorous class hatred – that this recognition, I say, came to me at the hands of an enemy – of a rank Prussian.

THE LADY: You don't say so!

AUGUSTUS: How else should I be here instead of starving to death in Ruhleben? Yes, Madam: the Colonel of the Pomeranian regiment which captured me, after learning what I had done, and conversing for an hour with me on European politics and military strategy, declared that nothing would induce him to deprive my country of my services, and set me free. I offered, of course, to procure the release in exchange of a German officer of equal quality; but he would not hear of it. He was kind enough to say he could not believe that a German officer answering to that description existed. (*With emotion.*) I had my first taste of the ingratitude of my own country as I made my way back to our lines. A shot from our front trench struck me in the head. I still carry the flattened projectile as a trophy. (*He throws it on the table: the noise it makes testifies to its weight.*) Had it penetrated to the brain I might never have sat on another Royal Commission. Fortunately we have strong heads, we Highcastles. Nothing has ever penetrated to our brains.

THE LADY: How thrilling! How simple! And how tragic! But you will forgive England? Remember: England! Forgive her.

AUGUSTUS (*with gloomy magnanimity*): It will make no difference whatever to my services to my country. Though she slay me, yet will I, if not exactly trust her, at least take my part in her government. I am ever at my country's call. Whether it be the embassy in a leading European capital, a governor-generalship in the tropics, or my humble mission here to make Little Pifflington do its bit, I am always ready for the sacrifice. Whilst England remains England, wherever there is a public job to be done you will find a Highcastle sticking to it. And now, Madam enough of my tragic personal history. You have called on business. What can I do for you?

THE LADY: You have relatives at the Foreign Office, have you not?

AUGUSTUS (*haughtily*): Madam: the Foreign Office is staffed by my relatives exclusively.

THE LADY: Has the Foreign Office warned you that you are being pursued by a female spy who is determined to obtain possession of a certain list of gun emplacements —

AUGUSTUS (*interrupting her somewhat loftily*): All that is perfectly well known to this department, Madam.

THE LADY (*surprised and rather indignant*): Is it? Who told you? Was it one of your German brothers-in-law?

AUGUSTUS (*injured, remonstrating*): I have only three German brothers-in-law, Madam. Really, from your tone, one would suppose that I had several. Pardon my sensitiveness on that subject; but reports are continually being circulated that I have been shot as a traitor in the courtyard of the Ritz Hotel simply because I have German brothers-in-law. (*With feeling.*) If you had a German brother-in-law, Madam, you would know that nothing else in the world produces so strong an anti-German feeling. Life affords no keener pleasure than finding a brother-in-law's name in the German casualty list.

THE LADY: Nobody knows that better than I. Wait until you hear what I have come to tell you: you will understand me as no one else could. Listen. This spy, this woman —

AUGUSTUS (*all attention*): Yes?

THE LADY: She is a German. A Hun.

AUGUSTUS: Yes, yes. She would be. Continue.

THE LADY: She is my sister-in-law.

AUGUSTUS (*deferentially*): I see you are well connected, Madam. Proceed.

THE LADY: Need I add that she is my bitterest enemy?

AUGUSTUS: May I — (*He proffers his hand. They shake, fervently. From this moment onward* AUGUSTUS *becomes more and more confidential, gallant, and charming.*)

THE LADY: Quite so. Well, she is an intimate friend of your brother at the War Office, Hungerford Highcastle: Blueloo as you call him: I don't know why.

AUGUSTUS (*explaining*): He was originally called The Singing Oyster, because he sang drawing-room ballads with such an extraordinary absence of expression. He was then called the Blue Point for a season or two. Finally he became Blueloo.

THE LADY: Oh, indeed: I didn't know. Well, Blueloo is simply infatuated with my sister-in-law; and he has rashly let out to her that this list is in your possession. He forgot himself because he was in a towering rage at its being entrusted to you: his language was terrible. He ordered all the guns to be shifted at once.

AUGUSTUS: What on earth did he do that for?

THE LADY: I can't imagine. But this I know. She made a bet with him that she would come down here and obtain possession of that list and get clean away into the street with it. He took the bet on condition that she brought it straight back to him at the War Office.

AUGUSTUS: Good heavens! And you mean to tell me that Blueloo

F

was such a dolt as to believe that she could succeed? Does he take me for a fool?

THE LADY: Oh, impossible! He is jealous of your intellect. The bet is an insult to you: don't you feel that? After what you have done for our country —

AUGUSTUS: Oh, never mind that. It is the idiocy of the thing I look at. He'll lose his bet; and serve him right!

THE LADY: You feel sure you will be able to resist the siren? I warn you she is very fascinating.

AUGUSTUS: You need have no fear, Madam. I hope she will come and try it on. Fascination is a game that two can play at. For centuries the younger sons of the Highcastles have had nothing to do but fascinate attractive females when they were not sitting on Royal Commissions or on duty at Knightsbridge barracks. By Gad, Madam, if the siren comes here she will meet her match.

THE LADY: I feel that. But if she fails to seduce you —

AUGUSTUS (*blushing*): Madam!

THE LADY (*continuing*): – from your allegiance —

AUGUSTUS: Oh, that!

THE LADY: – she will resort to fraud, to force, to anything. She will burgle your office: she will have you attacked and gar-rotted at night in the street.

AUGUSTUS: Pooh! I'm not afraid.

THE LADY: Oh, your courage will only tempt you into danger. She may get the list after all. It is true that the guns are moved. But she would win her bet.

AUGUSTUS (*cautiously*): You did not say that the guns were moved. You said that Blueloo had ordered them to be moved.

THE LADY: Well, that is the same thing, isn't it?

AUGUSTUS: Not quite – at the War Office. No doubt those guns will be moved: possibly even before the end of the war.

THE LADY: Then you think they are there still! But if the German War Office gets the list – and she will copy it before she gives it back to Blueloo, you may depend on it – all is lost.

AUGUSTUS (*lazily*): Well, I should not go as far as that. (*Lowering his voice.*) Will you swear to me not to repeat what I am going to say to you; for if the British public knew that I had said it, I should be at once hounded down as a pro-German.

THE LADY: I will be silent as the grave. I swear it.

AUGUSTUS (*again taking it easily*): Well, our people have for some reason made up their minds that the German War Office is everything that our War Office is not – that it carries promptitude, efficiency, and organization to a pitch of completeness and perfection that must be, in my opinion, destructive to the happiness of the staff. My own view – which you are pledged, remember, not to betray – is that the German War Office is no better than any other War Office. I found that opinion on my observation of the characters of my brothers-in-law: one of whom, by the way, is on the German general staff. I am not at all sure that this list of gun emplacements would receive the smallest attention. You see, there are always so many more important things to be attended to. Family matters, and so on, you understand.

THE LADY: Still, if a question were asked in the House of Commons —

AUGUSTUS: The great advantage of being at war, Madam, is that nobody takes the slightest notice of the House of Commons. No doubt it is sometimes necessary for a Minister to soothe the more seditious members of that assembly by giving a pledge or two; but the War Office takes no notice of such things.

THE LADY (*staring at him*): Then you think this list of gun emplacements doesn't matter!!

AUGUSTUS: By no means, Madam. It matters very much indeed. If this spy were to obtain possession of the list, Blueloo would tell the story at every dinner-table in London; and —

THE LADY: And you might lose your post. Of course.

AUGUSTUS (*amazed and indignant*): *I* lose my post! What are you dreaming about, Madam? How could I possibly be spared? There are hardly Highcastles enough at present to fill half the posts created by this war. No: Blueloo would not go that far.

He is at least a gentleman. But I should be chaffed; and, frankly, I don't like being chaffed.

THE LADY: Of course not. Who does? It would never do. Oh never, never.

AUGUSTUS: I'm glad you see it in that light. And now, as a measure of security, I shall put that list in my pocket. (*He begins searching vainly from drawer to drawer in the writing-table.*) Where on earth —? What the dickens did I —? That's very odd: I – Where the deuce —? I thought I had put it in the — Oh, here it is! No: this is Lucy's last letter.

THE LADY (*elegiacally*): Lucy's Last Letter! What a title for a picture play!

AUGUSTUS (*delighted*): Yes: it is, isn't it? Lucy appeals to the imagination like no other woman. By the way (*Handing over the letter.*) I wonder could you read it for me? Lucy is a darling girl; but I really can't read her writing. In London I get the office typist to decipher it and make me a typed copy; but here there is nobody.

THE LADY (*puzzling over it*): It is really almost illegible. I think the beginning is meant for 'Dearest Gus'.

AUGUSTUS (*eagerly*): Yes: that is what she usually calls me. Please go on.

THE LADY (*trying to decipher it*): 'What a' – 'what a' – oh yes: 'what a forgetful old' – something – 'you are!' I can't make out the word.

AUGUSTUS (*greatly interested*): Is it blighter? That is a favourite expression of hers.

THE LADY: I think so. At all events it begins with a B. (*Reading.*) 'What a forgetful old' – (*She is interrupted by a knock at the door.*)

AUGUSTUS (*impatiently*): Come in. (THE CLERK *enters, clean shaven and in khaki, with an official paper and an envelope in his hand.*) What is this ridiculous mummery, sir?

THE CLERK (*coming to the table and exhibiting his uniform to both*): They've passed me. The recruiting officer come for me. I've had my two and seven.

AUGUSTUS (*rising wrathfully*): I shall not permit it. What do they mean by taking my office staff? Good God! they will be taking our hunt servants next. (*Confronting the clerk.*) What did the man mean? What did he say?

THE CLERK: He said that now you was on the job we'd want another million men, and he was going to take the old-age pensioners or anyone he could get.

AUGUSTUS: And did you dare knock at my door and interrupt my business with this lady to repeat this man's ineptitudes?

THE CLERK: No. I come because the waiter from the hotel brought this paper. You left it on the coffee-room breakfast-table this morning.

THE LADY (*intercepting it*): It is the list. Good heavens!

THE CLERK (*proffering the envelope*): He says he thinks this is the envelope belonging to it.

THE LADY (*snatching the envelope also*): Yes! Addressed to you. Lord Augustus! (AUGUSTUS *comes back to the table to look at it.*) Oh, how imprudent! Everybody would guess its importance with your name on it. Fortunately I have some letters of my own here (*Opening her wallet.*) Why not hide it in one of my envelopes? then no one will dream that the enclosure is of any political value. (*Taking out a letter, she crosses the room towards the window, whispering to Augustus as she passes him.*) Get rid of that man.

AUGUSTUS (*haughtily approaching the clerk, who humourously makes a paralytic attempt to stand at attention*): Have you any further business here, pray?

THE CLERK: Am I to give the waiter anything; or will you do it yourself?

AUGUSTUS: Which waiter is it? The English one?

THE CLERK: No: the one that calls hisself a Swiss. Shouldn't wonder if he'd made a copy of that paper.

AUGUSTUS: Keep your impertinent surmises to yourself, sir. Remember that you are in the army now; and let me have no more of your civilian insubordination. Attention! Left turn! Quick march!

THE CLERK (*stolidly*): I dunno what you mean.

AUGUSTUS: Go to the guard-room and report yourself for diso-
beying orders. Now do you know what I mean?

THE CLERK: Now look here. I ain't going to argue with you —

AUGUSTUS: Nor I with you. Out with you.

He seizes the clerk, and rushes him through the door. The moment THE
LADY *is left alone, she snatches a sheet of official paper from the
stationery rack; folds it so that it resembles the list; compares the two
to see that they look exactly alike; whips the list into her wallet; and
substitutes the facsimile for it. Then she listens for the return of
Augustus. A crash is heard, as of the clerk falling downstairs.*

AUGUSTUS *returns and is about to close the door when the voice of the
clerk is heard from below:*

THE CLERK: I'll have the law of you for this, I will.

AUGUSTUS (*shouting down to him*): There's no more law for you,
you scoundrel. You're a soldier now. (*He shuts the door and
comes to the lady.*) Thank heaven, the war has given us the upper
hand of these fellows at last. Excuse my violence; but disci-
pline is absolutely necessary in dealing with the lower middle
classes.

THE LADY: Serve the insolent creature right! Look! I have
found you a beautiful envelope for the list, an unmistakable
lady's envelope. (*She puts the sham list into her envelope and hands
it to him.*)

AUGUSTUS: Excellent. Really very clever of you. (*Slyly.*) Come:
would you like to have a peep at the list? (*Beginning to take the
blank paper from the envelope.*)

THE LADY (*on the brink of detection*): No no. Oh, please, no.

AUGUSTUS: Why? It won't bite you (*Drawing it out farther.*)

THE LADY (*snatching at his hand*): Stop. Remember: if there should
be an inquiry, you must be able to swear that you never showed
that list to a mortal soul.

AUGUSTUS: Oh, that is a mere form. If you are really curious —

THE LADY: I am not. I couldn't bear to look at it. One of my
dearest friends was blown to pieces by an aircraft gun; and
since then I have never been able to think of one without
horror.

AUGUSTUS: You mean it was a real gun, and actually went off. How sad! how sad! (*He pushes the sham list back into the envelope, and pockets it.*)

THE LADY: Ah! (*Great sigh of relief.*) And now, Lord Augustus, I have taken up too much of your valuable time. Goodbye.

AUGUSTUS: What! Must you go?

THE LADY: You are so busy.

AUGUSTUS: Yes; but not before lunch, you know. I never can do much before lunch. And I'm no good at all in the afternoon. From five to six is my real working time. Must you really go?

THE LADY: I must, really. I have done my business very satisfactorily. Thank you ever so much. (*She proffers her hand.*)

AUGUSTUS (*shaking it affectionately as he leads her to the door, but first pressing the bell button with his left hand*): Goodbye. Goodbye. So sorry to lose you. Kind of you to come; but there was no real danger. You see, my dear little lady, all this talk about war saving, and secrecy, and keeping the blinds down at night, and so forth, is all very well; but unless it's carried out with intelligence, believe me, you may waste a pound to save a penny; you may let out all sorts of secrets to the enemy; you may guide the Zeppelins right on to your own chimneys. That's where the ability of the governing class comes in. Shall the fellow call a taxi for you?

THE LADY: No, thanks: I prefer walking. Goodbye. Again, many, many thanks.

She goes out. AUGUSTUS *returns to the writing-table smiling, and takes another look at himself in the mirror.* THE CLERK *returns with his head bandaged, carrying a poker.*

THE CLERK: What did you ring for? (AUGUSTUS *hastily drops the mirror.*) Don't you come nigh me or I'll split your head with this poker, thick as it is.

AUGUSTUS: It does not seem to me an exceptionally thick poker. I rang for you to show the lady out.

THE CLERK: She's gone. She run out like a rabbit. I ask myself, why was she in such a hurry?

THE LADY'S VOICE (*from the street*): Lord Augustus. Lord Augustus.

THE CLERK: She's calling you.

AUGUSTUS (*running to the window and throwing it up*): What is it? Won't you come up?

THE LADY: Is the clerk there?

AUGUSTUS: Yes. Do you want him?

THE LADY: Yes.

AUGUSTUS: The lady wants you at the window.

THE CLERK (*rushing to the window and putting down the poker*): Yes, Maam? Here I am, Maam. What is it, Maam?

THE LADY: I want you to witness that I got clean away into the street. I am coming up now.

The two men stare at one another.

THE CLERK: Wants me to witness that she got clean away into the street!

AUGUSTUS: What on earth does she mean?

The lady returns.

THE LADY: May I use your telephone?

AUGUSTUS: Certainly. Certainly. (*Taking the receiver down.*) What number shall I get you?

THE LADY: The War Office, please.

AUGUSTUS: The War Office!?

THE LADY: If you will be so good.

AUGUSTUS: But — Oh, very well. (*Into the receiver.*) Hallo. This is the Town Hall Recruiting Office. Give me Colonel Bogey, sharp.

A pause.

THE CLERK (*breaking the painful silence*): I don't think I'm awake. This is a dream of a movy picture, this is.

AUGUSTUS (*his ear at the receiver*): Shut up, will you? (*Into the telephone.*) What? . . . (*To the lady.*) Whom do you want to get on to?

THE LADY: Blueloo.

AUGUSTUS (*into the telephone*): Put me through to Lord Hungerford Highcastle. . . . I'm his brother, idiot. . . . That you,

Blueloo? Lady here at Little Pifflington wants to speak to you. Hold the line. (*To the lady.*) Now, Madam (*He hands her the receiver.*)

THE LADY (*sitting down in Augustus's chair to speak into the telephone.*) Is that Blueloo? . . . Do you recognize my voice? . . . I've won our bet. . . .

AUGUSTUS: Your bet!

THE LADY (*into the telephone*): Yes: I have the list in my wallet. . . .

AUGUSTUS: Nothing of the kind, Madam. I have it here in my pocket. (*He takes the envelope from his pocket; draws out the paper; and unfolds it.*)

THE LADY (*continuing*): Yes: I got clean into the street with it. I have a witness. I could have got to London with it. Augustus won't deny it. . . .

AUGUSTUS (*contemplating the blank paper*): There's nothing written on this. Where is the list of guns?

THE LADY (*continuing*): Oh, it was quite easy. I said I was my sister-in-law and that I was a Hun. He lapped it up like a kitten. . . .

AUGUSTUS: You don't mean to say that —

THE LADY (*continuing*): I got hold of the list for a moment and changed it for a piece of paper out of his stationery rack: it was quite easy. (*She laughs; and it is clear that Blueloo is laughing too.*)

AUGUSTUS: What!

THE CLERK (*laughing slowly and laboriously, with intense enjoyment*): Ha ha! Ha ha ha! Ha! (AUGUSTUS *rushes at him: he snatches up the poker and stands on guard.*) No you don't.

THE LADY (*still at the telephone, waving her disengaged hand behind her impatiently at them to stop making a noise*): Sh-sh-sh-sh-sh!!! (AUGUSTUS, *with a shrug, goes up the middle of the room.* THE LADY *resumes her conversation with the telephone.*) What? . . . Oh yes: I'm coming up by the 12.35: why not have tea with me at Rumpel-meister's . . . Rum-pelmeister's. You know: they call it Robinson's now. . . . Right. Ta ta. (*She hangs up the receiver, and is passing round the table on her way towards the door when she is confronted by Augustus.*)

AUGUSTUS: Madam: I consider your conduct most unpatriotic. You make bets and abuse the confidence of the hard-worked officials who are doing their bit for their country whilst our gallant fellows are perishing in the trenches —

THE LADY: Oh, the gallant fellows are not all in the trenches, Augustus. Some of them have come home for a few days hard-earned leave; and I am sure you won't grudge them a little fun at your expense.

THE CLERK: Hear! Hear!

AUGUSTUS (*amiably*): Ah, well! For my country's sake —!

Annajanska, The Bolshevik Empress

A Revolutionary Romancelet

When a comedy is performed, it is nothing to me that
the spectators laugh; any fool can make an audience laugh.
I want to see how many of them, laughing or grave, are
in the melting mood. And this result cannot be achieved,
even by actors who thoroughly understand my purpose,
except through an artistic beauty of execution unattainable
without long and arduous practice, and an intellectual
effort which my plays probably do not seem serious
enough to call forth.

CHARACTERS

ANNAJANSKA, *the Grand Duchess*
GENERAL STRAMMFEST
LIEUTENANT SCHNEIDEKIND
TWO SOLDIERS

SCENE: The General's Office at an army station on the Eastern Front, Beotia.

TIME: October 1917.

The play was first produced at the London Coliseum on 21 January 1918 with Lillah McCarthy in the title role.

ANNAJANSKA, THE BOLSHEVIK EMPRESS

This is very much a play of its period. In 1917 the First World War was at its height and the fighting was at its toughest. In Russia (the Beotia of the play) the October Revolution had brought the Bolsheviks to power. Here in the play current events are moving too swiftly for the old General, an aristocrat of the old school. Not only is there political instability and insecurity, with the ruling Panjandrum (i.e. the Czar) deposed, but a member of the royal house has defected to the side of the revolutionaries. This is a typical Shavian situation; he revelled in giving his audiences situations that were seemingly contradictory, with roles reversed.

A successful performance of this play will depend almost entirely on the skill of the actress playing Annajanska. Shaw himself called it 'a bravura piece'; it was written specially to enable a talented actress of the period (Lillah McCarthy*) to take part in a variety bill at the London Coliseum in January 1918. Here is yet another proof of Shaw's versatility; he saw himself in a new role fresh from the awful legitimacy of the highbrow theatre'.

If what Shaw tells us is true the original script of *Annajanska* was shorter than the printed text. He deliberately – typically one might say – added a page or two more to make it longer after a friend complimented him on the fact that unlike his other plays this one was 'not too long'. But, of course, Shaw quite often wrote thus with his tongue in his cheek.

The setting is as straightforward as that in any play by Shaw. The General's Office should present no problem. In the original production use was made of Tschaikowsky's '1812 Overture' as background music; it seems as good a choice as any.

The original Lavinia in *Androcles and the Lion*.

ANNAJANSKA, THE BOLSHEVIK EMPRESS

The General's Office in a military station on the east front in Beotia. An office table with a telephone, writing materials, official papers, etc., is set across the room. At the end of the table, a comfortable chair for the General. Behind the chair, a window. Facing it at the other end of the table, a plain wooden bench. At the side of the table, with its back to the door, a common chair, with a typewriter before it. Beside the door, which is opposite the end of the bench, a rack for caps and coats. There is nobody in the room.

General Strammfest enters, followed by Lieutenant Schneidekind. They hang up their cloaks and caps, Schneidekind takes a little longer than Strammfest, who comes to the table.

STRAMMFEST: Schneidekind.

SCHNEIDEKIND: Yes, sir.

STRAMMFEST: Have you sent my report yet to the government? (*He sits down.*)

SCHNEIDEKIND (*coming to the table*): Not yet, sir. Which government do you wish it sent to? (*He sits down.*)

STRAMMFEST: That depends. What's the latest? Which of them do you think is most likely to be in power tomorrow morning?

SCHNEIDEKIND: Well, the provisional government was going strong yesterday. But today they say that the prime minister has shot himself, and that the extreme left fellow has shot all the others.

STRAMMFEST: Yes: that's all very well; but these fellows always shoot themselves with blank cartridge.

SCHNEIDEKIND: Still, even the blank cartridge means backing down. I should send the report to the Maximilianists.

STRAMMFEST: They're no stronger than the Oppidoshavians; and in my own opinion the Moderate Red Revolutionaries are as likely to come out on top as either of them.

SCHNEIDEKIND: I can easily put a few carbon sheets in the typewriter and send a copy each to the lot.

STRAMMFEST: Waste of paper. You might as well send reports to an infant school. (*He throws his head on the table with a groan.*)

SCHNEIDEKIND: Tired out, sir?

STRAMMFEST: O Schneidekind, Schneidekind, how can you bear to live?

SCHNEIDEKIND: At my age, sir, I ask myself how can I bear to die?

STRAMMFEST: You are young, young and heartless. You are excited by the revolution: you are attached to abstract things like liberty. But my family has served the Panjandrums of Beotia faithfully for seven centuries. The Panjandrums have kept our place for us at their courts, honoured us, promoted us, shed their glory on us, made us what we are. When I hear you young men declaring that you are fighting for civilization, for democracy, for the overthrow of militarism, I ask myself how can a man shed his blood for empty words used by vulgar tradesmen and common labourers: mere wind and stink. (*He rises, exalted by his theme.*) A king is a splendid reality, a man raised above us like a god. You can see him; you can kiss his hand; you can be cheered by his smile and terrified by his frown. I would have died for my Panjandrum as my father died for his father. Your toiling millions were only too honoured to receive the toes of our boots in the proper spot for them when they displeased their betters. And now what is left in life for me? (*He relapses into his chair discouraged.*) My Panjandrum is deposed and transported to herd with convicts. The army, his pride and glory, is paraded to hear seditious speeches from penniless rebels, with the colonel actually forced to take the chair and introduce the speaker. I myself am made Commander-in-Chief by my own solicitor: a Jew, Schneidekind! a Hebrew Jew! It seems only yesterday that these things would have been the ravings of a madman: today they are the common-places of the gutter press. I live now for three objects only: to defeat the enemy, to restore the Panjandrum, and to hang my solicitor.

SCHNEIDEKIND: Be careful, sir: these are dangerous views to utter nowadays. What if I were to betray you?

STRAMMFEST: What!

SCHNEIDEKIND: I won't, of course; my own father goes on just like that; but suppose I did?

STRAMMFEST (*chuckling*): I should accuse you of treason to the Revolution, my lad; and they would immediately shoot you, unless you cried and asked to see your mother before you died, when they would probably change their minds and make you a brigadier. Enough. (*He rises and expands his chest.*) I feel the better for letting myself go. To business. (*He takes up a telegram; opens it; and is thunderstruck by its contents.*) Great heaven! (*He collapses into his chair.*) This is the worst blow of all.

SCHNEIDEKIND: What has happened? Are we beaten?

STRAMMFEST: Man: do you think that a mere defeat could strike me down as this news does: I, who have been defeated thirteen times since the war began? O, my master, my master, my Panjandrum! (*He is convulsed with sobs.*)

SCHNEIDEKIND: They have killed him?

STRAMMFEST: A dagger has been struck through his heart —

SCHNEIDEKIND: Good God!

STRAMMFEST: – and through mine, through mine.

SCHNEIDEKIND (*relieved*): Oh: a metaphorical dagger. I thought you meant a real one. What has happened?

STRAMMFEST: His daughter, the Grand Duchess Annajanska, she whom the Panjandrina loved beyond all her other children, has – has — (*He cannot finish.*)

SCHNEIDEKIND: Committed suicide?

STRAMMFEST: No. Better if she had. Oh, far far better.

SCHNEIDEKIND (*in hushed tones*): Left the Church?

STRAMMFEST (*shocked*): Certainly not. Do not blaspheme, young man.

SCHNEIDEKIND: Asked for the vote?

STRAMMFEST: I would have given it to her with both hands to save her from this.

SCHNEIDEKIND: Save her from what? Dash it, sir, out with it.

STRAMMFEST: She has joined the Revolution.

SCHNEIDEKIND: But so have you, sir. We've all joined the Revolution. She doesn't mean it any more than we do.

STRAMMFEST: Heaven grant you may be right! But that is not the worst. She has eloped with a young officer. Eloped, Schneidekind, eloped!

SCHNEIDEKIND (*not particularly impressed*): Yes, sir.

STRAMMFEST: Annajanska, the beautiful, the innocent, my master's daughter! (*He buries his face in his hands.*)
The telephone rings.

SCHNEIDEKIND (*taking the receiver*): Yes: G.H.Q. Yes. . . . Don't bawl: I'm not a general. Who is it speaking? . . . Why didn't you say so? don't you know your duty? Next time you will lose your stripe. . . . Oh, they've made you a colonel, have they? Well, they've made me a field-marshal: now what have you to say? . . . Look here: what did you ring up for? I can't spend the day here listening to your cheek. . . . What! the Grand Duchess! (STRAMMFEST *starts.*) Where did you catch her?

STRAMMFEST (*snatching the telephone and listening for the answer*): Speak louder, will you: I am a General. . . . I know that, you dolt. Have you captured the officer that was with her? . . . Damnation! You shall answer for this: you let him go: he bribed you. . . . You must have seen him: the fellow is in the full dress court uniform of the Panderobajensky Hussars. I give you twelve hours to catch him or . . . what's that you say about the devil? Are you swearing at me, you . . . Thousand thunders! (*To Schneidekind.*) The swine says that the Grand Duchess is a devil incarnate. (*Into the telephone.*) Filthy traitor: is that the way you dare speak of the daughter of our anointed Panjandrum? I'll —

G

SCHNEIDEKIND (*pulling the telephone from his lips*): Take care, sir.

STRAMMFEST: I won't take care: I'll have him shot. Let go that telephone.

SCHNEIDEKIND: But for her own sake, sir —

STRAMMFEST: Eh?

SCHNEIDEKIND: For her own sake they had better send her here. She will be safe in your hands.

STRAMMFEST (*yielding the receiver*): You are right. Be civil to him. I should choke. (*He sits down.*)

SCHNEIDEKIND (*into the telephone*): Hullo. Never mind all that: it's only a fellow here who has been fooling with the telephone. I had to leave the room for a moment. Wash out; and send the girl along. We'll jolly soon teach her to behave herself here. . . . Oh, you've sent her already. Then why the devil didn't you say so, you — (*He hangs up the telephone angrily.*) Just fancy: they started her off this morning: and all this is because the fellow likes to get on the telephone and hear himself talk now that he is a colonel. (*The telephone rings again. He snatches the receiver furiously.*) What's the matter now? . . . (*To the General.*) It's our own people downstairs. (*Into the receiver.*) Here! do you suppose I've nothing else to do than to hang on to the telephone all day? . . . What's that? Not men enough to hold her! What do you mean? (*To the General.*) She is there, sir.

STRAMMFEST: Tell them to send her up. I shall have to receive her without even rising, without kissing her hand, to keep up appearances before the escort. It will break my heart.

SCHNEIDEKIND (*into the receiver*): Send her up. . . . Tcha! (*He hangs up the receiver.*) He says she is half-way up already: they couldn't hold her.

THE GRAND DUCHESS *bursts into the room, dragging with her two exhausted soldiers hanging on desperately to her arms. She is enveloped from head to foot by a fur-lined cloak, and wears a fur cap.*

SCHNEIDEKIND (*pointing to the bench*): At the word Go, place your prisoner on the bench in a sitting posture; and take your seats right and left of her. Go.

THE TWO SOLDIERS *make a supreme effort to force her to sit down.*

She flings them back so that they are forced to sit on the bench to save themselves from falling backwards over it, and is herself dragged into sitting between them. THE SECOND SOLDIER, *holding on tight to* THE GRAND DUCHESS *with one hand, produces papers with the other, and waves them towards* SCHNEIDEKIND, *who takes them from him and passes them on to the General. He opens them and reads them with a grave expression.*

SCHNEIDEKIND: Be good enough to wait, prisoner, until the General has read the papers on your case.

THE GRAND DUCHESS (*to the soldiers*): Let go. (*To Strammfest.*) Tell them to let go, or I'll upset the bench backwards and bash our three heads on the floor.

FIRST SOLDIER: No, little mother. Have mercy on the poor.

STRAMMFEST (*growling over the edge of the paper he is reading*): Hold your tongue.

THE GRAND DUCHESS (*blazing*): Me, or the soldier?

STRAMMFEST (*horrified*): The soldier, Madam.

THE GRAND DUCHESS: Tell him to let go.

STRAMMFEST: Release the lady.

THE SOLDIERS *take their hands off her. One of them wipes his fevered brow. The other sucks his wrist.*

SCHNEIDEKIND (*fiercely*): 'ttention!

THE TWO SOLDIERS *sit up stiffly.*

THE GRAND DUCHESS: Oh, let the poor man suck his wrist. It may be poisoned. I bit it.

STRAMMFEST (*shocked*): You bit a common soldier!

THE GRAND DUCHESS: Well, I offered to cauterize it with the poker in the office stove. But he was afraid. What more could I do?

SCHNEIDEKIND: Why did you bite him, prisoner?

THE GRAND DUCHESS: He would not let go.

STRAMMFEST: Did he let go when you bit him?

THE GRAND DUCHESS: No. (*Patting the soldier on the back.*) You should give the man a cross for his devotion. I could not go on eating him; so I brought him along with me.

STRAMMFEST: Prisoner —

THE GRAND DUCHESS: Don't call me prisoner, General Strammfest. My grandmother dandled you on her knee.

STRAMMFEST (*bursting into tears*): O God, yes. Believe me, my heart is what it was then.

THE GRAND DUCHESS: Your brain also is what it was then. I will not be addressed by you as prisoner.

STRAMMFEST: I may not, for your own sake, call you by your rightful and most sacred titles. What am I to call you?

THE GRAND DUCHESS: The Revolution has made us comrades. Call me comrade.

STRAMMFEST: I had rather die.

THE GRAND DUCHESS: Then call me Annajanska; and I will call you Peter Piper, as grandmamma did.

STRAMMFEST (*painfully agitated*): Schneidekind: you must speak to her: I cannot — (*He breaks down.*)

SCHNEIDEKIND (*officially*): The Republic of Beotia has been compelled to confine the Panjandrum and his family, for their own safety, within certain bounds. You have broken those bounds.

STRAMMFEST (*taking the word from him*): You are – I must say it – a prisoner. What am I to do with you?

THE GRAND DUCHESS: You should have thought of that before you arrested me.

STRAMMFEST: Come, come, prisoner! do you know what will happen to you if you compel me to take a sterner tone with you?

THE GRAND DUCHESS: No. But I know what will happen to you.

STRAMMFEST: Pray what, prisoner?

THE GRAND DUCHESS: Clergyman's sore throat.

SCHNEIDEKIND *splutters: drops a paper; and conceals his laughter under the table.*

STRAMMFEST (*thunderously*): Lieutenant Schneidekind.

SCHNEIDEKIND (*in a stifled voice*): Yes, sir. (*The table vibrates visibly.*)

STRAMMFEST: Come out of it, you fool: you're upsetting the

ink. SCHNEIDEKIND *emerges, red in the face with suppressed mirth.*

STRAMMFEST: Why don't you laugh? Don't you appreciate Her Imperial Highness's joke?

SCHNEIDEKIND (*suddenly becoming solemn*): I don't want to, sir.

STRAMMFEST: Laugh at once, sir. I order you to laugh.

SCHNEIDEKIND (*with a touch of temper*): I really can't, sir. (*He sits down decisively.*)

STRAMMFEST (*growling at him*): Yah! (*He turns impressively to the Grand Duchess.*) Your Imperial Highness desires me to address you as comrade?

THE GRAND DUCHESS (*rising and waving a red handkerchief*): Long live the Revolution, comrade!

STRAMMFEST (*rising and saluting*): Proletarians of all lands, unite. Lieutenant Schneidekind: you will rise and sing the Marseillaise.

SCHNEIDEKIND (*rising*): But I cannot, sir. I have no voice, no ear.

STRAMMFEST: Then sit down; and bury your shame in your typewriter (SCHNEIDEKIND *sits down.*) Comrade Annajanska: you have eloped with a young officer.

THE GRAND DUCHESS (*astounded*): General Strammfest: you lie.

STRAMMFEST: Denial, comrade, is useless. It is through that officer that your movements have been traced. (THE GRAND DUCHESS *is suddenly enlightened, and seems amused.* STRAMMFEST *continues in a forensic manner.*) He joined you at the Golden Anchor in Hakonsburg. You gave us the slip there; but the officer was traced to Potterdam, where you rejoined him and went alone to Premsylople. What have you done with that unhappy young man? Where is he?

THE GRAND DUCHESS (*pretending to whisper an important secret*): Where he has always been.

STRAMMFEST (*eagerly*): Where is that?

THE GRAND DUCHESS (*impetuously*): In your imagination. I came alone. I am alone. Hundreds of officers travel every day from Hakonsburg to Potterdam. What do I know about them?

STRAMMFEST: They travel in khaki. They do not travel in full dress court uniform as this man did.

SCHNEIDEKIND: Only officers who are eloping with grand duchesses wear court uniform: otherwise the grand duchesses could not be seen with them.

STRAMMFEST: Hold your tongue. (SCHNEIDEKIND, *in high dudgeon, folds his arms and retires from the conversation.* THE GENERAL *returns to his paper and to his examination of the Grand Duchess.*) This officer travelled with your passport. What have you to say to that?

THE GRAND DUCHESS: Bosh! How could a man travel with a woman's passport?

STRAMMFEST: It is quite simple, as you very well know. A dozen travellers arrive at the boundary. The official collects their passports. He counts twelve persons; then counts the passports. If there are twelve, he is satisfied.

THE GRAND DUCHESS: Then how do you know that one of the passports was mine?

STRAMMFEST: A waiter at the Potterdam Hotel looked at the officer's passport when he was in his bath. It was your passport.

THE GRAND DUCHESS: Stuff! Why did he not have me arrested?

STRAMMFEST: When the waiter returned to the hotel with the police the officer had vanished; and you were there with your own passport. They knouted him.

THE GRAND DUCHESS: Oh! Strammfest: send these men away. I must speak to you alone.

STRAMMFEST (*rising in horror*): No: this is the last straw: I cannot consent. It is impossible, utterly, eternally impossible, that a daughter of the Imperial House should speak to anyone alone, were it even her own husband.

THE GRAND DUCHESS: You forget that there is an exception. She may speak to a child alone. (*She rises.*) Strammfest: you have been dandled on my Grandmother's knee. By that gracious action the dowager Panjandrina made you a child forever. So did Nature, by the way. I order you to speak to me alone. Do you hear? I order you. For seven hundred years no member of your family has ever disobeyed an order from a member of mine. Will you disobey me?

STRAMMFEST: There is an alternative to obedience. The dead cannot disobey. (*He takes out his pistol and places the muzzle against his temple.*)

SCHNEIDEKIND (*snatching the pistol from him*): For God's sake, General —

STRAMMFEST (*attacking him furiously to recover the weapon*): Dog of a subaltern, restore that pistol, and my honour.

SCHNEIDEKIND (*reaching out with the pistol to the Grand Duchess*): Take it: quick: he is as strong as a bull.

THE GRAND DUCHESS (*snatching it*): Aha! Leave the room, all of you except the General. At the double! lightning! electricity! (*She fires shot after shot, spattering bullets about the ankles of the soldiers. They fly precipitately. She turns to Schneidekind, who has by this time been flung on the floor by the General.*) You too. (*He scrambles up.*) March. (*He flies to the door.*)

SCHNEIDEKIND (*turning at the door*): For your own sake, comrade —

THE GRAND DUCHESS (*indignantly*): Comrade! You!!! Go. (*She fires two more shots. He vanishes.*)

STRAMMFEST (*making an impulsive movement towards her*): My Imperial Mistress —

THE GRAND DUCHESS: Stop. I have one bullet left, if you attempt to take this from me. (*Putting the pistol to her temple.*)

STRAMMFEST (*recoiling, and covering his eyes with his hands*): No no: put it down: put it down. I promise everything: I swear anything; put it down, I implore you.

THE GRAND DUCHESS (*throwing it on the table*): There!

STRAMMFEST (*uncovering his eyes*): Thank God!

THE GRAND DUCHESS (*gently*): Strammfest: I am your comrade. Am I nothing more to you?

STRAMMFEST (*falling on his knee*): You are, God help me, all that is left to me of the only power I recognize on earth. (*He kisses her hand.*)

THE GRAND DUCHESS (*indulgently*): Idolater! When will you learn that our strength has never been in ourselves, but in your illusions about us? (*She shakes off her kindliness, and sits down in his chair.*) Now tell me, what are your orders? And do you mean to obey them?

STRAMMFEST (*starting like a goaded ox, and blundering fretfully about the room*): How can I obey six different dictators, and not one gentleman among the lot of them? One of them orders me to make peace with the foreign enemy. Another orders me to offer all the neutral countries forty-eight hours to choose between adopting his views on the single tax and being instantly invaded and annihilated. A third orders me to go to a damned Socialist Conference and explain that Beotia will allow no annexations and no indemnities, and merely wishes to establish the Kingdom of Heaven on Earth throughout the universe. (*He finishes behind Schneidekind's chair.*)

THE GRAND DUCHESS: Damn their trifling!

STRAMMFEST: I thank Your Imperial Highness from the bottom of my heart for that expression. Europe thanks you.

THE GRAND DUCHESS: M'yes; but — (*Rising.*) Strammfest: you know that your cause – the cause of the dynasty – is lost.

STRAMMFEST: You must not say so. It is treason, even from you. (*He sinks, discouraged, into the chair, and covers his face with his hand.*)

THE GRAND DUCHESS: Do not deceive yourself, General: never again will a Panjandrum reign in Beotia. (*She walks slowly across the room, brooding bitterly, and thinking aloud.*) We are so decayed, so out of date, so feeble, so wicked in our own despite, that we have come at last to will our own destruction.

STRAMMFEST: You are uttering blasphemy.

THE GRAND DUCHESS: All great truths begin as blasphemies. All the king's horses and all the king's men cannot set up my father's throne again. If they could, you would have done it, would you not?

STRAMMFEST: God knows I would!

THE GRAND DUCHESS: You really mean that? You would

keep the people in their hopeless squalid misery? you would fill those infamous prisons again with the noblest spirits in the land? you would thrust the rising sun of liberty back into the sea of blood from which it has risen? And all because there was in the middle of the dirt and ugliness and horror a little patch of court splendour in which you could stand with a few orders on your uniform, and yawn day after day and night after night in unspeakable boredom until your grave yawned wider still, and you fell into it because you had nothing better to do. How can you be so stupid, so heartless?

STRAMMFEST: You must be mad to think of royalty in such a way. I never yawned at court. The dogs yawned; but that was because they were dogs: they had no imagination, no ideals, no sense of honour and dignity to sustain them.

THE GRAND DUCHESS: My poor Strammfest: you were not often enough at court to tire of it. You were mostly soldiering; and when you came home to have a new order pinned on your breast, your happiness came through looking at my father and mother and at me, and adoring us. Was that not so?

STRAMMFEST: Do you reproach me with it? I am not ashamed of it.

THE GRAND DUCHESS: Oh, it was all very well for you, Strammfest. But think of me, of me! standing there for you to gape at, and knowing that I was no goddess, but only a girl like any other girl! It was cruelty to animals: you could have stuck up a wax doll or a golden calf to worship; it would not have been bored.

STRAMMFEST: Stop; or I shall renounce my allegiance to you. I have had women flogged for such seditious chatter as this.

THE GRAND DUCHESS: Do not provoke me to send a bullet through your head for reminding me of it.

STRAMMFEST: You always had low tastes. You are no true daughter of the Panjandrums: you are a changeling, thrust into the Panjandrina's bed by some profligate nurse. I have heard stories of your childhood: of how —

THE GRAND DUCHESS: Ha, ha! Yes: they took me to the

circus when I was a child. It was my first moment of happiness, my first glimpse of heaven. I ran away and joined the troupe. They caught me and dragged me back to my gilded cage; but I had tasted freedom; and they never could make me forget it.

STRAMMFEST: Freedom! To be the slave of an acrobat! to be exhibited to the public! to —

THE GRAND DUCHESS: Oh, I was trained to that. I had learnt that part of the business at court.

STRAMMFEST: You had not been taught to strip yourself half naked and turn head over heels —

THE GRAND DUCHESS: Man: I wanted to get rid of my swaddling clothes and turn head over heels. I wanted to, I wanted to, I wanted to. I can do it still. Shall I do it now?

STRAMMFEST: If you do, I swear I will throw myself from the window so that I may meet your parents in heaven without having my medals torn from my breast by them.

THE GRAND DUCHESS: Oh, you are incorrigible. You are mad, infatuated. You will not believe that we royal divinities are mere common flesh and blood even when we step down from our pedestals and tell you ourselves what a fool you are. I will argue no more with you: I will use my power. At a word from me your men will turn against you: already half of them do not salute you; and you dare not punish them: you have to pretend not to notice it.

STRAMMFEST: It is not for you to taunt me with that if it is so.

THE GRAND DUCHESS (*haughtily*): Taunt! *I* condescend to taunt! To taunt a common General! You forget yourself, sir.

STRAMMFEST (*dropping on his knee submissively*): Now at last you speak like your royal self.

THE GRAND DUCHESS: Oh, Strammfest, Strammfest, they have driven your slavery into your very bones. Why did you not spit in my face?

STRAMMFEST (*rising with a shudder*): God forbid!

THE GRAND DUCHESS: Well, since you will be my slave, take your orders from me. I have not come here to save our wretched family and our bloodstained crown. I am come to save the Revolution.

STRAMMFEST: Stupid as I am, I have come to think that I had better save that than save nothing. But what will the Revolution do for the people? Do not be deceived by the fine speeches of the revolutionary leaders and the pamphlets of the revolutionary writers. How much liberty is there where they have gained the upper hand? Are they not hanging, shooting, imprisoning as much as ever we did? Do they ever tell the people the truth? No: if the truth does not suit them they spread lies instead, and make it a crime to tell the truth.

THE GRAND DUCHESS: Of course they do. Why should they not?

STRAMMFEST (*hardly able to believe his ears*): Why should they not!

THE GRAND DUCHESS: Yes: why should they not? We did it. You did it, whip in hand: you flogged women for teaching children to read.

STRAMMFEST: To read sedition. To read Karl Marx.

THE GRAND DUCHESS: Pshaw! How could they learn to read the Bible without learning to read Karl Marx? Why do you not stand to your guns and justify what you did, instead of making silly excuses. Do you suppose *I* think flogging a woman worse than flogging a man? I, who am a woman myself!

STRAMMFEST: I am at a loss to understand your Imperial Highness. You seem to me to contradict yourself.

THE GRAND DUCHESS: Nonsense! I say that if the people cannot govern themselves, they must be governed by somebody. If they will not do their duty without being half forced and half humbugged, somebody must force them and humbug them. Some energetic and capable minority must always be in power. Well, I am on the side of the energetic minority whose principles I agree with. The Revolution is as cruel as we were; but its aims are my aims. Therefore I stand for the Revolution.

STRAMMFEST: You do not know what you are saying. This is pure Bolshevism. Are you, the daughter of a Panjandrum, a Bolshevist?

THE GRAND DUCHESS: I am anything that will make the world less like a prison and more like a circus.

STRAMMFEST: Ah! You still want to be a circus star.

THE GRAND DUCHESS: Yes, and be billed as the Bolshevik Empress. Nothing shall stop me. You have your orders, General Strammfest: save the Revolution.

STRAMMFEST: What Revolution? Which Revolution? No two of your rabble of revolutionists mean the same thing by the Revolution. What can save a mob in which every man is rushing in a different direction?

THE GRAND DUCHESS: I will tell you. The war can save it.

STRAMMFEST: The war?

THE GRAND DUCHESS: Yes, the war. Only a great common danger and a great common duty can unite us and weld these wrangling factions into a solid commonwealth.

STRAMMFEST: Bravo! War sets everything right: I have always said so. But what is a united people without a united army? And what can *I* do? I am only a soldier. I cannot make speeches: I have won no victories: they will not rally to my call (*again he sinks into his chair with his former gesture of discouragement*).

THE GRAND DUCHESS: Are you sure they will not rally to mine?

STRAMMFEST: Oh, if only you were a man and a soldier!

THE GRAND DUCHESS: Suppose I find you a man and a soldier?

STRAMMFEST (*rising in a fury*): Ah! the scoundrel you eloped with! You think you will shove this fellow into an army command, over my head. Never.

THE GRAND DUCHESS: You promised everything. You swore anything. (*She marches as if in front of a regiment.*) I know that this man alone can rouse the army to enthusiasm.

STRAMMFEST: Delusion! Folly! He is some circus acrobat; and you are in love with him.

THE GRAND DUCHESS: I swear I am not in love with him. I swear I will never marry him.

STRAMMFEST: Then who is he?

THE GRAND DUCHESS: Anybody in the world but you would have guessed long ago. He is under your very eyes.

STRAMMFEST (*staring past her right and left*): Where?

THE GRAND DUCHESS: Look out of the window.

He rushes to the window, looking for the officer. THE GRAND DUCHESS *takes off her cloak and appears in the uniform of the Panderobajensky Hussars.*

STRAMMFEST (*peering through the window*): Where is he? I can see no one.

THE GRAND DUCHESS: Here, silly.

STRAMMFEST (*turning*): You! Great Heavens! The Bolshevik Empress!